DEATH AT SOMBRERO ROCK

Red Ant and his Comanche warriors rode down from the Mountains of Death to raid along the Texas border and bring destruction to isolated homesteads. But they reckon without one man, former US Deputy Marshal, Black Pete Bowen. All Pete wants is to live peacefully with his beautiful young wife, Louisa, and their son. But he is forced to take the war to the enemy, and, crossing the Rio Grande, he attacks Mexican bandits who are supplying the Indians with whiskey and guns.

Greedy neighbours, dirty tricks, falling cattle prices, and the temptation of Louisa by his handsome best friend while he is away, are other problems Pete has to handle in this story of violence and jealousy which lead inexorably to a tragic holocaust of leaping flames.

Death at Sombrero Rock

JOHN DYSON

A Black Horse Western

ROBERT HALE · LONDON

Photoset in North Wales by
Derek Doyle & Associates, Mold, Clwyd.
Printed in Great Britain by
St Edmundsbury Press Ltd, Bury St Edmunds, Suffolk.
Bound by WBC Bookbinders Ltd, Bridgend, Glamorgan.

ONE

'Lone rider coming,' a hand called.

And he was coming fast. The shrill, panicked shout from the look-out had set everybody's neck turning and their fingers reaching for their guns. They could see the cloud of dust as he came hell for leather around the edge of Sombrero Rock quirting his mount from side to side as it came down the rise, stumbling, but regaining its feet, and coming on across the flat of purple sage towards the ranch house.

And they heard the sound that chilled the spine, that froze the blood even in the southern Texas heat, an ullulating chant of wild voices raised in unison, the voices of death, the voices of Comanches who had been burning and scalping and raiding all the way along the border. They were coming round the rock charging after him.

'He ain't goin' to make it.'

'Yes, he is.'

The rider, unfamiliar with the terrain, had taken a slight semi-circular curve, but the Comanche, superb horsemen, were speeding across the rocks of the hillside on a narrow trail intent on intercepting him. Their voices were exultantly raised in expectation of the kill.

'Open the gate!'

'He ain't going to make it.'

'He sure will,' Black Pete muttered.

He had run out to take his place by the rough stockade built around the log ranch buildings. There was only one thing to do: hit out the leading Comanche horse. He raised his Winchester, this year's model, a '73 and squinted along the sights, taking it slowly, coolly – now! The leading Indian pony collapsed, bringing others behind it tumbling into a melée of dust and enraged howls.

'Got you,' he whispered.

His bullet must have penetrated the horse's lung for it had gone down whinnying and kicking its last. It gave the lone rider time to come thundering on at a gallop, kicking his spurs, hung low, his Mexican sombrero brim flattened back by the speed, by the wind; scrambling to the dust as he got through the gate, which was quickly closed, and the pursuing savages were stopped in their tracks by a fusillade of shots from the cowhands who had come running....

'Git back in the house, Jim,' the tall man with the Winchester shouted to his eight-year-old son who was eagerly firing off his own rifle. 'Look after your mother.'

'It's Red Ant,' the boy shrilled, peering into the dust at the Indians, who were gesticulating and screaming, rearing their horses, and letting fly with lances, bows, and carbines.

'All the more reason for you to get in,' Pete called back. 'Do as I say, boy.'

Jim backed away, anxiously watching, as one of the Comanches, his hair feathered and his body painted for war, decided he was impervious to lead, and charged at a weak portion of the fence, clearing it in a flying leap, yelling in his trance of fate.

The Indian hurled his scalp-hung lance at Frank, the foreman, who had run up from the far corral. It went clean through him, pinning him with a thunk to the log wall.

The boy saw the Indian, a tomahawk in his other hand, coming on towards him. For moments he froze, then, gritting his teeth, he pressed the trigger of his small calibre rifle. He had only brought down a jack rabbit before, but the lead ball was big enough to topple the brave off his horse, and send him spinning across the ground.

As the painted horse careered past him the youngster stared transfixed at the wounded Indian who was trying to raise himself, trying to reach his knife.

'Ahh-hee!' the Comanche cried, his fierce eyes intense. Was this the final insult, to be brought down by a small white boy? Must he give him his spirit? As a bullet caught him in the back his eyes clouded and he slumped.

'For God's sake get in,' Pete shouted.

'Jim!' his mother was screaming from the porch.

The boy stared at the Indian. He had never killed a man before; stared at his rifle in his hands; heard his father's shouts, his mother's screams; and he hesitated, snatched at the warrior's scalp-hung tomahawk before he was scooped up in his mother's arms.

Pete turned back to the fray. The Comanches were less than fifty yards away, firing and making suicidal rushes at the white men. Pete fired angrily, pulling down the trigger lever with

practised control, and dislodged at least five of the
marauders before his magazine was empty.

Amid the plumes of dust and shouts of death
and battle, the harsh whinnying of horses, the
thrashing of wounded animals and fallen men,
the brittle scent of fired carbines, he dodged down
to reload and met the fiercely blue eyes of the
stranger who had sought refuge.

A strange sensation passed through him in
those few seconds in the lull of battle. The rider
was dressed in the Mexican manner, the tight
embroidered trousers, cruel spurs and leather
jacket. His face was dark, but delicately drawn,
and his sombrero had fallen back from a matted
dust-mop of curls. He gave a shy grin as he, too,
reloaded an ancient Navy Colt, and as he looked
into his blue eyes Pete knew that he had met
either a friend or an enemy. Or, perhaps, both.

But, he hadn't much time to think about that,
because on his other side he saw an arrow thud
into the chest of one of his best hands, Jem, and
saw him go down.

And through the red dust, close to, on the other
side of the barricade, he could see the Comanche
who had fired it, who before Pete could finish
reloading, had another arrow fitted to his bow. He
wore a red disc banded to the centre of his
forehead, and a springing crest of bristles on top
of his knotted hair. His body was painted with
ochre striations. It was Red Ant. And his arrow
was aimed their way.

Pete hurled himself at the stranger, knocking
him aside, as the arrow hissed across their backs.
'Shee-it,' he growled, his hand on the stranger's
shoulder, peering up. 'If I'd a had one more slug

left I coulda got him.'

It was too late. Red Ant and the Comanches were retreating, picking up their wounded and racing off. Soon they became a cloud of dust disappearing into the landscape of distances. That was the way they fought: hit and run. Sometimes they would lay waste the settlement they attacked, leaving it a burning ruin on the plain. This time they hadn't had the luck.

The tall young man, Pete Bowen, owner of the Wild Rose ranch by settler's claim, scraped his fingers through his thick black hair and looked about him at the sudden devastation and death that had been brought about. A half-hour before it had been a peaceful Sunday morning and he had been enjoying a late lie-in with his wife, taking coffee and other comforts, when the warning had been called. They had near been caught unawares.

'Hot damn. Where'n hell did they come from? On the Sabbath, too. It jest ain't civilized.'

The stranger laughed, possibly from relief. 'You sure don' expect them heathen to call for a quiet prayer meeting? Anyhows, thank the great Jesus, I thought I was a gonner. It seem like mirage when I see your little house.'

'Mebbe it was meant to be,' Pete muttered, and, meeting once again the clear flinty-blue eyes, wondered why he should speak thus. He suddenly realized he hadn't had time to put on his boots or brace of guns. He was standing there in a worn and faded pair of jeans, barefoot, and bare-chested. His upper body was leanly muscled and sun-tanned. He looked something like an Indian, himself, his eyes dark and sharp as thorns, only he wore a thick black moustache, which no Indian did. 'Them durn savages,' he said. 'I'm gonna have ta do somethun 'bout this.'

He knelt down beside the man with the arrow in his chest. Jem had broken off the shaft in his writhings to get it out. The head was buried deep in his lung.

'Ahm done fer,' Jem said.

'Not yet you ain't,' Pete told him.

His wife, Louisa, a Spanish girl, her eyes and hair as dark as his own, had run out, closely followed by young Jim.

'What can I do for him?' she asked.

'Not a lot,' Pete muttered, turning away. 'No way I can operate with a knife. In too deep. Probably pizened, too. Try to get him in the shade. Careful as you can. I'm goin' after them.'

'No!' Louisa screamed. 'Let them go.'

Pete hesitated; his eyes narrowed. 'They ain't gittin' away with none of my cows, nor my hosses. Any of you boys comin' along?'

'There ain't many of us left,' said Matthew, an older man. 'Frank's gone to meet his Maker. Andy caught lead in his eye: kilt in an instant. The best way. Clay, there, got an arrow in his arm. There's two to bury, and' – he glanced at Jem – 'another one soon by the looks of things. Thet only leaves us five and the two Mex farm boys, who ain't much good in a fight.'

'Red Ant's runnin', ain't he?' Pete snarled. 'We gotta keep him runnin'. Show him it ain't wise to mess us about.'

He stalked into the house, the house he had built in this wild valley, this corner of south-west Texas, with his own hands. No damn Comanch' was going to drive him out.

He pulled on his boots, his shotgun chaps, a black wool shirt, and red bandanna, and was fixing his spurs and his twin Smith and Wesson .44s, stashing them handles-forward in his belt when the stranger appeared.

'How about you?'

'My horse is tuckered in. I'm thirsty, myself.'

'Help yourself. Coffee on the stove. How about if I find you a fresh mount?'

'I just escaped the scalp-hungry clutches of those savages. Didn't figure on giving them another chance at my hair.'

Pete jammed his sweat-stained stetson on his head, slung a bandoleer of bullets across his shoulders. 'Where you from?'

The young man poured himself a coffee from the pot, appraised Pete once again with his ice-cool eyes, took a sip of the scalding brew before he spoke 'Mexico.'

'Yeah, I gathered that. You speak good English for a Mex. Where'bouts you from?'

'Comalcalo. Ramojad. Been in San Luis Potosi, seeking silver there. Couple of weeks ago was in Cerralvo. But mostly, these past months, I been hanging out at the Canyon Diablo.'

Pete looked up sharply. 'What doin'?'

'Ah.' The man threw off his wide-brimmed sombrero, ladled water over his matt of curls, wiped his forehead. 'Got mixed-in with some *bandidos* down there. The name El Zapote mean anything to you?'

One of the Smith and Wessons appeared in Pete's right hand and he covered the man. 'Comancheros?'

The stranger had his back turned and hadn't noticed the gun. 'That's what they call them.'

'It's you bin supplyin' these Comanch' with carbines.'

'Hey,' the stranger said, turning round, fanning out his palms. 'What's all this? It was Zapote doing the gun-running. I was jest helping out, making a few dollars.'

'We string up Comancheros this side the border.'

'Come on. We been trading with the Indians for a hundred years. It is not exactly new.'

Pete eyed him, quizzically, and reholstered his gun. Maybe he could make use of this man.

'If it weren't for El Zapote Red Ant would think twice before attacking us. Those men wouldn't be lying dead out there.'

'Well, I am a Comanchero no more. Got tired of their scurvy ways. Man didn't feel safe. So I come north of the border to see what America like.'

Louisa was ushering the men in carrying Jem, insisting they lay him on her marital bed. He was breathing bad and blood was trickling from his mouth.

'If anythin' happen,' she said to him, 'is there anybody we tell?'

'My sister in Deep Springs. Tell her ... tell her I fought brave.'

'You did, Jem,' she soothed him. 'You were always a good hand. I mean, don' you worry. You'll be all right.'

'I'm done for, ma'am,' he whispered. 'I know that.'

The other men entered the ranch house, excitedly discussing the battle, making claims as to how many Comanches they had de-horsed. Louisa went to cleaning Clay's wounded arm, giving the soothing female touch to him, too.

Pete, meanwhile, stomped about on the hard mud floor, looking dark and sullen and mean. Maybe that was why some folks called him Black Pete. He wanted to get on the trail, but was somehow reluctant to. He was angry that his wife was upset with him for wanting to go.

'Hail,' he said. 'Mebbe if these men had some vittles it would put some fire in their guts. Louisa, can you rustle them somethun' up? I'll be in the stable.'

'He don' mean no harm,' Louisa smiled at them, a Spanish lilt to her voice. 'Pete jest worry about his herd. You all did good. Young man, you pass that coffee round. Tortilla and beans good enough for you boys?'

'Sure Miz Bowen. Mighty fahn,' Matthew said. 'Don't you worry. He won't be goin' lone. I'll be with him for one.'

'Me, to,' said the stranger. 'Guess I'd better see to my poor horse. Don't eat it all while I'm gone.'

The other men muttered that they, too, would be riding out with Pete just as soon as they had got their second wind and had a bite.

Jim followed the Mexican to the stable where his father was saddling his big black stallion, Nimrod.

'Gee, Pa, wasn't it excitin'? Can I keep this tomahawk? That's the first Injun I killed.'

Pete looked at him severely. 'It ain't nuthin' to be proud of, killin' people. Not at your age. I told you to go inside. Next time I give you an order you better obey it, pronto.'

The stranger saw Jim's face fall. He tousled his hair, and drawled, 'That was real fast thinkin' and fast shootin'. Wow! I couldn't have done it better myself.'

'You keep your nose out of my affairs.'

'C'mon, you curmudgeonly bastard,' – the stranger gave a flashing smile – 'tell your boy he did good. Reckon he takes after you. You a good shot, yourself.'

Pete turned to him. 'We Bowens sure don't give no second helpings. You better remember that.'

'We sure don't.' The boy whooped and jumped his legs up around Pete's waist, hanging on.

Pete hugged his son, spun him around, and sat him on Nimrod. 'Take him out into the yard nice 'n' easy. This feller's right. It was durn fine shootin', son.'

'C'mon, Nimrod,' the boy shouted, and clattered him out. 'We going to go after Red Ant.'

The stranger went to sponging down his bronc. It was all lathered up and looked like it could do with a little rest. 'By the way, we all decided to come along. Hope our friend Red Ant won't be waiting in ambush.'

'It's us who's going to ambush him,' Pete said. 'You can take that sorrel. She's a good horse.'

The curly-haired Mexican slung his saddle over the sorrel. 'Been having a lot of trouble with the redman?'

'They bin fightin' you Spaniards for 400 years and us for nigh on forty. They ain't eager to give up. I guess I cain't blame 'em. Us whites comin' in and takin' their land.'

'That's the way it goes. Guess they took it from somebody years ago.'

'It ain't jest them. It's you durn Comancheros. You come up from Mexico supplying them with whiskey, guns, ammo. How we ever goin' to pacify the Comanch'?'

'I tell you, I am not one no more.'

'Yeah, you know how many homesteads like this been burned down this last two years? A hundred; more. To tell you the truth, friend, I'm feared for my wife and boy. Been thinking of sending 'em back to Corpus Christi to stay with her father.'

'Something tells me from what I've seen of your wife and son' – the Mexican laughed – 'they wouldn't go.'

'Mebbe you're right,' Pete mused. 'What's your handle?'

'Don Estevan Ochoa, *señor*. At your service.'

'Pleased to meetcha, Estevan.'

TWO

'I been thinkin', boys,' Pete said, as he shook some tobacco from his pouch, licked his tongue along the paper's edge and neatly twirled a cigarette. 'Mebbe it's best to let 'em believe we ain't in pursuit. So there ain't no hurry. We got some buryin' to be done.'

He took a match from a slim silver box his wife had given him – his most precious possession after his guns – studied a naked lady painted in enamel on its side, struck a light, inhaled, and tossed his pouch to them to help themselves. He rocked his rocker on his boot heels and grinned at his weatherbeaten cowhands. 'Mebbe we can give Red Ant a surprise. I wancha to take the moccasins offen the dead redskins. Stuff 'em with dry grass to make 'em more comfortable. We might have some walking to do.'

The men groaned. If there was one thing a cowboy hated it was getting off his horse. The four hands were squatted on the dried mud floor of the ranch house main living-room and kitchen. He had offered the spare chair to Matthew, who had now become foreman. The Mexican leaned against the log wall finishing his beans.

'There's three or four dead ponies,' Pete said. 'I

want 'em butchered and dried 'fore the vultures git 'em. They don't make bad eatin',' – again the men groaned – 'sure better than slaughterin' my cows. I'm gonna need everyone I got for the trek north. As you know, things ain't been going too good.'

'Them durn Murchisons,' Matthew muttered. 'I reckon they're behind the rustlin', not the Indians. Comanch' ain't got no use fer cows. 'Cept fer a quick snack.'

'Who are they?' Estevan asked.

'Old Man Murchison owns the land on t'other side of them mountains,' – Pete nodded out of the door at a range of blue hills – 'Los Muertos they call em. All the land as far as you can ride for three days. He reckons because he fought in the Mexican War he's got the right to ride roughshod over everybody in these parts. He didn't like me moving into this unexplored valley and taking on the Comanch'. The greedy old buzzard figures it's rightly his.'

'But you don't.'

'People got a certain amount of respect and awe for the old man,' Matthew said. 'Anyhow's he spends most of his time in San Antone these days at that fancy Cattlemen's Club. It's them two sneakin' cowardly sons of his I don't like.'

Pete removed a strand of tobacco from his lip, flicked the cigarette butt out of the door. 'The old man brought them up to be the low-down rattlesnakes they are. He knows what's goin' on. He still calls the shots.'

He stood, a harsh, hard look on his face. 'One of these days there's gonna be a showdown.' He stalked out into the yard with his long ambling

stride, savagely pulled out the lance that was
pinning his ex-foreman Frank to the stable wall
and let him fall prostrate. 'He was a good man,' he
said.

The dead Comanche was laid out, his face a
frozen mask, painted for war. Scalps decorated
the knees of his leggings. He had killed many
whites. Around his neck were twirled wampum
beads, and the skull of an eagle hung from an ear
lobe. His black hair was braided in plaits. His
porcupine quill breastplate was bloodily shattered. It had been no protection against lead.

'These'll do me,' Pete said, pulling off his beaded
moccasins. He hefted the brave across Nimrod's
shoulders, and swung into the saddle. 'We'll take
their dead out to Sombrero Rock. The coyotes can
have 'em. I'll read a few words over our'n.'

'Paw!' Jim came running up. 'They've killed the
pigs in the paddock. Got so many arrows in 'em
they look like porky pincushions. You should see.'

Black Pete shook his head, sadly, as his stallion
pranced and arched his neck, eager to be away.
'Now thet kinda behaviour's jest plumb unfriendly. If they ain't careful them Comanches gonna
git me mad.'

THREE

The sun, a burning red lozenge, was sinking
behind Los Muertos range, and the shadow of
Sombrero Rock was lengthening across the plain.
The men had ridden off after the Comanches. The
two Mexican boys were butchering the meat,
hanging the hides to dry. Jim was practising
throwing his tomahawk at the stable door. Only
the occasional lonesome howl of a coyote, the
snicker of a mustang in the corral, broke the
silence. Louisa took some warm milk and bread
into Jem and tried to persuade him to eat. He was
breathing heavily, cold sweat pricking out on his
face. He shook his head. 'I'm done for,' he
whispered. 'I'm headin' fer Heaven's gate. You
reckern they'll let me in?'

'Sure He will,' Louisa said. 'But you ain't goin'
yet.'

As she lit the oil lamp her soft rounded cheeks
were suffused with a pink glow and the depths of
her dark eyes seemed to tremble with sympathy
for the dying man. A sensation of helplessness
came over her. There was so little she could do.
Sometimes she hated this harsh country.

From the shadow of the other room Clay stood
and watched her. He was an ugly-looking young

man; his hair thinly yellow, his moustache wispy; his head somehow too big for his small body, his short nose giving no impression of intelligence. He had not had much luck with women – what few there were on the frontier. Indeed, he had not been touched by one, or close to one, for seven months or so, since he had visited a whorehouse at Broken Bow – until that afternoon.

Clay licked his lips as he remembered the gentle touch of Louisa's fingers upon his arm as she dressed his wound, the tantalizing scent of her. Greedily he watched her moving lightly about the room, the litheness of her shapely rear in her swishing skirt, the velvety shadow of her bosom in the loose Spanish blouse, as she leaned to straighten the bedclothes. He scratched at his crotch. He felt as if he was going to burst, his whole body inflamed. He could not stop himself. His heart was beating madly. It was now or never. He went in and grabbed hold of her.

Louisa shrieked with surprise, fighting to get away from him as he pinned her against the wall and clawed at her breasts. He was panting and dribbling, lewdly, trying to kiss her, trying to put his hand up her skirt.

'Stop it, Clay,' she cried, wildly turning her face away to avoid his mouth.

But he was too strong for her, ripping her blouse apart, and dipping his head down to the warmth of her bare bosom, biting and slobbering as if he were demented.

'Hold it right there, you white trash,' a weak voice quavered, 'Or I'll blow a hole through what brain you ain't got.'

Clay had taken no account of the semi-conscious

man on the bed. Now he looked round into the eyehole of a Colt Frontier .45 which was being cocked. Jem's hold was wavering, but it was on him, no doubt about that.

Louisa thrust him off, her eyes fiery, and tried to cover herself. 'You get out. Pete will kill you for this, if he ever find out.'

'Drop your gunbelt first, you filthy varmint.'

Clay eyed, viciously, the weakened Jem and considered taking him, but took mind of his wounded arm and he did as he was bid, and the gunbelt clattered to the floor.

'What makes you think you so high and mighty, you Mex bitch? You wanted it. I knew you did, the way you touched me.'

'You' – Jem began to cough, a trickle of blood appearing at his mouth corner – 'you ain't fit to touch the hem of her dress. Louisa's got noble Spanish blood in her. And, apart from that, she … she's saintly.'

'All right, Jem,' – Louisa took the gun from his hand as he slumped back – 'thank you, you rest now. As for you, Clay, you're overwrought. I know it's hard for a young man out here on his own. I'm gonna try to forget what you done and said. But don' you ever try touch me again. Now get out of here. Get off our land. You can take a horse in lieu of wages.'

'Sure,' Clay slurred, backing out. 'We'll see 'bout that.'

Several rifles were propped against the wall as he passed, and he glanced at them out of his eye corner, but he didn't like the hellcat look of her, and stepped out into the dust and headed for the corral.

'Jim,' Louisa shouted. 'You get your rifle. Come
do what I tell you.'

The boy came running up as she watched Clay
rope and saddle a mustang. 'Whadja want, Ma?'

'You just be ready to shoot anybody I tell you.
You done it once today. You can do it again.'

Jim looked perplexed as Clay mounted up, 'You
goin' after Red Ant, Clay?' he called.

'Clay's leaving.'

'You ain't making me go through Douro Canyon
without my Colt?' Clay looked alarmed. 'What if I
run into Comanch'?'

Louisa emptied the revolver, tossed it to him,
with his ammunition belt. 'You take your
chances.'

'I ain't gonna fergit this, Miz Bowen.'

'Think yourself lucky,' she said, holding her
dress together, 'you are riding out of here. We
both goin' to forget it. Remember that.'

Clay savagely pulled the mustang's head round,
dug in his rowels, and pranced away across the
desolate plain towards the red-rimmed Los
Muertos and Douro Canyon. It crossed his mind,
maybe he could circle back in the dark, creep up
on them? They were only a woman, a kid, a dying
man, and two Mex's. But, his arm ached. He had
had enough for one day.

FOUR

A silver globe of moon had risen high making it easy enough to follow the Comanche tracks. Now, however, two sets of tracks had crossed, and Pete jumped down to examine them. 'That's the earlier set,' he said, pointing a finger.

'What makes you figure that?' Estevan asked.

'Take a look. There's ant tracks crossing the earlier prints. No sign of 'em on the more recent ones.'

'You must have hawk eyes, gringo. I can see nuthin'.'

Pete's teeth flashed a grin in the dusk. 'Stick around, you'll mebbe learn somethun. They ain't split up and gone separate ways, so they ain't reckoned on us followin'. And, lookee here, bloodstains. Thet's their wounded. Let's ride, boys.'

They pounded along in the semi-darkness, climbing up through a harsh country of high rocks and joshua trees, any of which might have been harbouring a hostile. But Pete reckoned the Indians would want to make the high ground before pitching camp. The tracks showed they were herding along some of his horses that had been left out to graze in Wild Rose valley.

The Comanche counted wealth in horses. The last time he had encountered one of their encampments Red Ant's father had shown him 400 he personally owned. The old buzzard had a tongue-twistin' Indian name and Pete had christened him Crazy About Horses. He had laughed and explained it to his tribe. That was two years back before present hostilities had commenced.

Pete remembered how he had ridden into their camp. It had taken some screwed-up nerve – he had been jumpy as a rabbit inside – but it was the only way. He had told them he was the new owner of Wild Rose valley. They could hunt and use his water. All he wanted from the land was the wild longhorns that roamed there. Maybe he could trade them white men's goods: pots and pans and iron implements. He and his family wished to be at peace with them. He told Crazy About Horses that white men would take this part of Texas sooner or later. Why not have as a neighbour one who wished to be a friend of the red man?

Red Ant had stood at a distance from the pow wow, haughty and handsome; his naked thighs strongly muscled; a live, red poisonous snake hanging around his neck; his hand gripped on a war club; his shining black braids curled in a topnot held by the strange crest and the red circular ornament which was tied by a filet of rawhide to his brow. His father had called out to him what Pete had to say, and he had grunted, arrogant, and looked away.

The uneasy peace had lasted for all of a year, and, then, like a prairie fire, the raids had flared up, licking their flames all along the border as the word spread and other tribes rode down from the Mountains of Death.

They had reached the entrance to an arroyo that led up into a high mesa. Many tracks crowded its sandy bottom. It was deathly quiet and well into the graveyard watch. Pete slipped from Nimrod and covered his nostrils with his gloved hand to calm him.

He signalled to the boys to do likewise. 'From here on we walk,' he muttered in a low voice. 'Git your spurs off and your moccasins on. We don't wanna make no sound.'

He sat in the shadow of the cliff, untying his *chaparejos* to make climbing easier, give his legs more freedom in a fight – or maybe if he had to run.

'I want my horses back,' he grunted to Estevan. 'There's a grey filly in that mob I was gentling along ready for Jim when his legs are stretched a bit.'

'How many you figure there are in their war party?'

'Only about twenty. Unless they've met up with more of their tribe. That's the chance we gotta take. I figure this arroyo leads to the top of the cliff. If we climb up the steep way that sure goin' to make 'em jump.'

'Well,' Estevan grinned, recklessly, so as not to show his fear. 'In Mexico we say the red man's like a wild bronc. The only way to tame him is to give him a good quirting when he bucks and misbehaves. Gradually he learns that it don't pay.'

'That's the way it's got to be,' Pete muttered, taking a swig from his canteen.

He stood, and said, 'Matthew, you stay here and look after the horses. If we ain't back by sun-up git the hell out.'

'Hail, I won't,' the older man growled. 'Durn hosses can be tied to the rocks. I ain't come all this way to miss a fight.'

'OK. Remember, boys, when I give the word we hit 'em hard with everything we got. We grab our horses. Me and Estevan will take the rearguard as you herd 'em down the arroyo. Then we git out fast. Let's move.'

And, climb they did, following Pete as he made his way up the steep almost impassable cliffside, stifling curses as they got spiked by cactus and sharp rocks, but generally succeeding to be as quiet as the Comanche themselves.

As they neared the top of the ridge Pete waved them to a halt. He had spied the shadowy silhouette of an Indian guard sat crouched in his blanket, feathers sloped in his hair, a rifle across his knees. His regard was aimed at the arroyo, the way he would have expected them to come, particularly a white man, who made a lot of noise, and lit big fires as if to advertise himself.

Pete put down his rifle, carefully slipped his Smith and Wessons out, laid them on a rock. He slid his bowie knife from its sheath and crept forward, silent as a snake. As the razor-sharp blade slit his jugular the brave only uttered a surprised grunt through Pete's gloved hand.

Estevan climbed up and gave Pete his guns. 'They're along there,' he whispered. 'You can just see the glow of their fire.'

Pete and the five men spread out, crouching,

and moved along the top of the wind-eroded platte. They could see the shadowy forms of the Comanches slumbering around the embers of their small fire. Pete heard a low guttural sound and, looking across, saw another guard crooning words to the mob of ponies. The Indian turned, saw the men, and gave a harsh howl, before Pete's rifle slug, fired from the hip, took him out.

Immediately the Comanche were awake, jumping, crouching into position, as if they had only been pretending to sleep, but Pete's men had the advantage, their repeating rifles cracking out, sending a dozen of the Indians to perdition.

Uttering a wild death cry some five of the aboriginals rushed at the white men, reckless of their bullets, brandishing clubs, axes, knives, and lances, engaging them in hand-to-hand combat.

The others retreated, the remaining six, Red Ant among them, firing their arrows, but obviously shocked by the unexpected ferocity of the attack, running to their horses, picking themselves out a mount, and leaping away to escape, unsure how many more white men might be coming.

Pete swung his rifle club in the midst of battle, smashing the jaw of a painted brave, laying him low, as another landed on his back, and they rolled over, wrestling each other for the Indian's knife, the savage countenance an inch from his own face. He seemed to remember the man from more friendly days. It was Kneeling Horse. But, he turned the blade and plunged it into his heart.

He got to one knee, jerked out his .44 and blasted a hole in another warrior who was about to tomahawk Matthew. The foreman looked up at Pete with a whistle of relief.

Estevan was on his knees battling with the last of the Comanche attackers alive. He had got the better of him, a hand in his face, and was about to give the Comanche the *coup de grâce* with his own tomahawk. Pete grabbed his wrist, and held it. 'He's our prisoner.'

Two of his cowhands were lying sprawled bloodily dead. The other two were breathing hard, standing ready for any more comers. Pete looked after the departing Red Ant. He raised his Winchester. One of the Indians had reached the edge of the ridge, and, instead of plunging into safety, had turned and reared his horse, waving his spear in defiance at the white invaders. Pete's unerring bullet toppled him from the saddle.

'They always got to be so damn cocky,' he said.

The cowboys looked around them. The plateau was deserted, its wild configurations running away in long grey ridges of uninhabited scrub and thorn bottom. Not a soul to be seen for miles. Somewhere out there were the Comanch'. And suddenly all the colours were changing to a rich copper red as a fireball of sun began to appear glimmering and smouldering from behind an easterly escarpment, its rays flashing and gesticulating, lighting up their battle-excited faces.

'You done well, boys. We give 'em a hiding. And we got our hosses back. You all right, Matt? That's a bad gash on your thigh. Let me wrap something round it.'

'It ain't so bad,' Matthew growled, peering at the blood trickling from his ripped trousers. 'It coulda bin lot worse. Thanks Mister Bowen. You saved my bacon that time.'

'Couldn't lose a good foreman, could I? Who's fer picking up our dead and gitting back home?'

'What'll we do with him?' Estevan asked, keeping a tight hold of the disarmed Indian.

'Now let's see.' Pete struggled to remember his Comanche words. 'You speak Red Ant he attack my rancho many more red men die. Savvy?' He pointed back towards the ranch. 'My valley, my horses, you hear? You speak Crazy About Horses that me, Pete, I want peace with red man. If not, long swords, come, kill you all. *Comprende*?'

The Comanche stared impassively through him, resigned to death. Pete picked up a carbine. 'Where you get this?'

There was no reply, so he smashed it on a rock. 'Aw, clear off, you dumb bastard. Go on. Vamoose.'

The Comanche got up, slowly backed away, then turned and ran bounding over the rocks like a deer towards the ridge. He turned once, gave a wolf howl of rage, and leapt away.

'You certainly done told him,' Matthew grinned. 'If it had been me I'd have strung him up as a warning. Speaks more than words. They don't like the hempen necktie.'

'Not many men do,' Pete replied.

It was high noon when Louisa saw a whirl of dust approaching across the plain and she studied it, uneasily, through the wavering mirage lines of heat. If it was Comanche there was little she could do to protect herself and Jim. Gradually, however, she saw that it was the men, and, again, her heart almost stopped to see two bodies slung across saddles, and experienced a leap of selfish joy as she recognized the long rangy lines of her

husband, his straightbacked way of sitting the big
black stallion.

She had married him when she was sixteen,
and he eighteen, shortly after he returned from
the ravages of the Civil War; a boy who had
become a man. Since then he had been away for
long spells, working as a ranch hand, and leading
cattle drives for three months up through Indian
country to the Kansas railheads. On the last of
these drives he had stayed on in Abilene to keep
law, and, promoted to US Deputy Marshal, had
spent four months tracking down a dangerous
half-breed. When Pete got on the trail of a man
there wasn't much short of an earthquake would
shake him off. And he had earned enough bounty
to set out on his heart's one ambition, to have a
ranch of his own. Sure, it was a hard life, but
Louisa wanted no other life. The Wild Rose ranch
was her home.

She ran to hug Pete around the waist as he
dismounted digging her fingers into his ribs. It
made her feel good to have him back again. Pete
gave a whoop and whisked her off her feet,
whirling her around. 'Told ya they wouldn't git my
hosses, didn't I? We got twelve of the varmints, to
our two.'

Louisa's face fell – guilty at being so happy.
'They were only boys.'

'They knew the score. You don't git no second
chances when it's hand-to-hand combat with the
Comanche. Somethun's gotta be done. We either
kill Red Ant, or El Zapote, or both, or they'll drive
us off.'

'Jem's passed on,' Louisa said.

'I guessed so,' Pete replied, entering the ranch

house, fondling the tousled hair of Jim, who had run to hug Pete from his other side.

'Where's Clay gotten to?' he called.

'Oh, he left.'

'On his own? What for?'

'He' – Louisa had never lied to her husband before and stumbled on the words – 'he said he'd had enough. I gave him one of the horses.'

Pete's dark eyes brooded on her for moments. 'Thet's kinda odd, ain't it?'

Louisa avoided his eyes and those of her son, who was looking up at her, anxiously. And she met the vivid blue ones of the copper-faced stranger, who was standing there in the doorway in his Mexican garments, a faint smile hovering on his lips, as if he could read her mind, and she blushed, furiously.

'It's like I said,' she cried. 'What you make fuss about? He wasn't no good that Clay. Bad rubbish.'

For some reason she shivered as Estevan continued to watch her, knowingly. It was as if he knew the reason for Clay's departure and as if his eyes, too, were undressing her.

As the sun began to go down they walked over to the small burial ground, which was fast getting bigger, on the hillside. Pete took off his hat and spoke about each of the boys by name, what little he knew of them. Now they lay beneath mounds of earth and stones to keep the coyotes off, with rough crosses at their heads. Pete looked across at the threatening silhouette of Los Muertos and shouted, ' "Vengeance is mine, sayeth the Lord". But this day I am the Lord, I repay.'

FIVE

In a makeshift forge alongside the stable Pete was fixing a wheel of the wagon, heating its iron rim with fire, holding it with tongs, hammering the nails home.

Estevan, in his skin-tight embroidered trousers, rowelled spurs and snakeskin jacket, was leaning, idly watching. 'You fixing on going some place?'

'Yup,' Pete grunted. 'Broken Bow. You wanna come along? Louisa needs some stores and I need some more men. I'm fast runnin' out.'

Jim whooped excitedly at the news and ran to tell his mother, and pretty soon, with Pete at the reins, and Estevan riding along, they were jingling and rattling across the plain. They got through the Douro Canyon without seeing any sign of hostiles, but, by mid-afternoon, as they were crossing the Murchisons' land, a bunch of riders hove into sight.

The leading rider, a cadaverous-faced hombre known as Slim McKenzie, who liked to go around in a black gambler's outfit, frock coat and stove pipe trousers, to show he was no ordinary cowhand, pulled up his mustang in a flurry of dust to block their way.

'Who gave you permission to cross Murchison land?'

The men behind him glowered at them, threateningly.

'How the hell else am I goin' get to town?'

'Mister Murchison don't want you Bowens on his land. You ain't got no right here.'

'I got as much right as he's got. Range rights.'

Pete had seen this man Slim strutting his stuff in the saloon at Broken Bow. He was Murchison's top hired gun. And he liked to let people know it. Seven men, at least, had caught lead poisoning from him when he found himself losing at cards and falsely accused them of cheating.

'Well, we say you ain't got no rights.'

'You aiming to stop me going to town?' Pete's hackles were rising. He jumped down from the wagon, so his wife and son wouldn't be in the firing line, and strode around the front of his horses to the gunman. 'You step down from that horse and I'll show you what rights I got man to man.'

Estevan moved his mount away from the wagon, and the men behind McKenzie smiled slightly at each other. Would Slim accept this invitation to settle the argument with fists? Or go for his gun? They knew he was fast, the fastest in the district. But they had heard that Bowen might just be faster.

'Let this be a warning to you, that's all. Mr Murchison don't want you in that valley. If I were you I would be strongly advised to take your family back to wherever you come from.'

'And if I were you I would strongly advise these men and the Murchisons to keep their hands off my cattle.'

'What you saying?' McKenzie cried. 'You hear that boys?'

'I'm saying I've had cattle gone missing and it ain't the Comanches.'

'He's got some damn nerve,' one of the 'punchers growled.

'Mebbe I'm making a mistake,' Pete drawled. 'But iffen I see any man runnin' off my herd the mistake's going to be a .44 calibre one.'

'C'mon, boys,' – McKenzie eyed the Smith and Wessons slung on Pete's hips and got the meaning – 'we've delivered the message. If this dunkhead cain't take good advice that's goin' t'be his bad luck. Heeyaugh! Let's move it.'

They turned their mustangs and went galloping away, and as Pete watched them go surging over a rise, he muttered, 'It's goin' t'be bad luck for one of us, that's for sure.'

The wagon went rattling and bouncing its way across the prairie, and, as they passed bunches of cattle, Pete glanced inquisitively at their brands. He didn't notice any with the Wild Rose insignia, or any sign of it. Maybe he was wrong. Maybe it was the Comanch' who had been running off his herd.

By mid-afternoon they arrived at the small township of Broken Bow, a haphazard collection of false-fronted plank stores, dry goods, saddlcry, bank, jailhouse, saloon, livery, a big ornate Spanish mission and a sprinkling of adobe Mexican houses.

By the way they loaded up the wagon with hundred-pound sacks of cornmeal, flour, sugar, chillies, baskets of lemons and so on, it should have been obvious to any onlooker that the

Bowens had no intention of willingly leaving their ranch.

And there were plenty of onlookers. Apart from settlers going about their business, there was a bunch of Mexican vaqueros, who leaned against the adobe walls. They looked like hard riders. Could they be some of El Zapote's men? And some of Murchison's men they had encountered on the plain came riding in, Slim McKenzie among them, who gave them hard looks before pushing through the batwing doors into the saloon. Behind the township rose the cold, hard, grey folds of Los Muertos mountains, haunt of Comanche and Comanchero.

While Louisa went to buy cloth for a new dress, and Jim to watch mustangs being broken in the town corral, Pete strolled over to the gun shop to stock up on bullets, and to the forge to pick out some ironware. As he did so he saw most of the Murchison mob go riding out back to their range.

Pete wasn't looking for trouble, but he had a dry throat, and, while he had discreetly avoided going into the saloon while Murchison's men were there, he figured it should be pretty quiet over there by now. He slapped Estevan on his shoulder and said, 'You ready for a beer or two, *amigo*.'

The saloon was a rough and ready joint, raised on a high sidewalk, made of unplaned planks. Pete narrowed his eyes, stepping into the shade from the sun's glare. There were some cowpokes lounged playing cards at makeshift tables and chairs at the far end, among them Slim McKenzie, who turned to watch them, snakelike, sticking out his long legs, and throwing back his black boxcoat to reveal a big Colt Frontier.

'Shee-it!' Pete growled – he thought he had gone – and he pretended not to notice two youngish men, who were engaged in some loud-mouthed horseplay at the bar: his un-neighbourly neighbours, the Murchison brothers. And they were well-whiskeyed up.

The barkeep stared venomously at Estevan, in his Mexican attire, his wide sombrero, and spurs rattling on the bare floorboards, as they went to the bar.

'Gimme a coupla beers,' Pete said.

The 'keep jerked his thumb at a scrawled notice behind him: *No Mex, Nigger or Injun served.*

'Thar's a cantina down by the corral for your sort.'

'You ever seen a Mexican with blue eyes?' Pete asked. 'Start pouring that beer.'

The older of the Murchisons, Hal, swung round to see what was going on, and realized through his haze who had arrived. He was a big bull-necked man, ham-fisted and fat-assed. One of those men who don't know the meaning of soft harmony. He had been used to giving orders since birth, and had had too much beef and buttermilk, and, latterly, liquor for his own good. One of those men whose shirt is constantly coming out of his pants; its neck tied with an angry, short necktie, ballooning taut at the front. At thirty he was already going bald and had a sour look.

The barkeep glanced at him, and hesitated.

'Do I git thet beer or not?' Pete said.

Hal leaned on the bar and sneered with drunken bravado, 'He don't serve saddle-tramps with greaser wives and half-breed brats. This is a gen'alman's club.'

At this, his brother, George, giggled. He was a skinnier version, used to being bullied by Hal, but, in his more natty attire of wide fringed chaps and piebald horsehair waistcoat, he, too, had a strutting cock-of-the-walk air. In this town, what these two ordered was done, pronto, and they knew it.

Pete had frozen, momentarily, at the insults to his wife and son, his gloved right hand on the point of reaching for his .44. But, a glance showed him they weren't armed. They had slung their gunbelts on a hook on the wall. However, Slim had slowly risen to his feet, and the men at the table quickly scrambled to one side.

'Keep outa this, McKenzie,' Pete said.

He went round the back of the bar and, with a hard shove, sent the barman staggering back against his bottles. Pete pulled a shotgun from under the bar, snapped it open and ejected the cartridges. He tossed it to one side. Slowly, he filled two glasses with beer, placed them before Estevan and went back to stand beside him. They slaked their thirst.

Pete slapped a silver dollar down on the bartop, and, like a flash as something snapped inside him, made a sideways swipe with his left arm, smashing his fist edge a hammerlike blow to Hal's nose, following around with a right uppercut to the point of his jaw that rocked him in his boots.

He staggered back, nearly flattening his brother. George helped him back on his feet. Hal shook his head like an angry bull, and, lowering it, charged at Pete, catching him full force, crashing him to the floor, trying to gouge out his eyes. Pete had the heavier man crushing him, his

thick fingers in his face, and, if it hadn't been for
Estevan giving Hal a quick kick to the side of the
head he wouldn't have got him off.

As he rolled Hal off, Pete got to his feet, keeping
an eye on McKenzie. George ran to hoist his
brother up again. As he did so Pete slammed in
another right, bouncing them both back against
the plank wall.

'Get him!' Hal roared, but Slim McKenzie had a
slight smile on his thin lips. He didn't like the look
of the curly-haired Mex who stood there, a
revolver holstered across his chest.

'It's your fight,' Slim said.

'Right, Bowen, you bastard' – Hal beckoned the
cowboy to him – 'you're goin' to regret this.'

He wanted to get on another bear-crush, but
Pete knew it was time to fight more scientific,
start sparring and feinting, dodging and moving,
the way Bear River Tom had taught him. He was
fit and agile and in his prime. He hadn't touched
whiskey since watching Blue Jay get hanged two
years before. His opponent was overweight and
already panting hard, swinging haymakers,
which Pete ducked.

But, it wasn't easy; Hal was crowding him in
the confined space, and his brother George was
swinging in ineffectual blows where he could. At
one point he got behind Pete and managed to hold
on to his arms while his brother, Hal, hit in hard
to Pete's right eye and mouth.

Estevan cured this by swinging George round,
and, with a smack of his fist, sent him tottering
back to collapse on to broken chairs at Slim's feet.
George shook his jaw with surprise, and decided
to stay down.

Estevan backed away, in case Slim tried anything, and Pete went all out to end it, swapping punches with Hal, making a bloody mess of his face, chopping him down like the brute he was. And he fell, groaning, to the floor, a felled ox.

Pete stood over him, his fists clenched. 'Want any more?' he shouted, and wiped the blood from his lip. His fists ached, and he eased them, hoping they weren't fractured. He had had to hit him hard enough. It looked like Hal might well have a broken nose.

'Get 'em outa here,' he said to Slim. 'And any time you want a meet let me know.'

Slim shrugged, and, with George, whose legs had gone kinda weak, hefted the semi-conscious rancher from the floor, dragged him out, and slung him, like a sack of meal, across his horse. They mounted up, and rode on out, the people looking at Hal's form, wonderingly. There would be trouble for this, most thought.

'Now are you goin' to serve us?' Pete asked the barkeep, straightening his clothes, tenderly touching his cut face. Estevan grinned, and one of the card-players, a short, stocky boy, with cropped fair hair, retrieved Pete's hat and dusted it off. 'Let me pay for that,' he said. 'I been longing for months to see that oaf git a whuppin'. Yassir.'

Pete winced, as this new boy, who gave his handle as Nathan, pumped his hand. 'Nathan Strong. I cain't abide them two. The old man ain't so bad. He's not goin' to like this. I worked fer him fer a while.'

'He should keep those boys in order. I blame Abraham Murchison for the way he's brought them up. They got what they call illusions of grand-door. They think they own Texas.'

'Waal, they do, a purty big patch. You're Mistuh Bowen, aincha? Used to call you Black Pete? I heard about ya in Abilene. You and that sexy little blonde, Molly, who turned Indian squaw. I hear she's ridin' with the Doolin gang now.'

'That so?' Pete said, somewhat startled, his past catching up. 'Little Moll, huh? She's quite a gal. But, that's somethun' I'd rather you didn't mention in these parts. I only got one gal, my wife.'

'Here's to Louisa,' Estevan said. 'You a bit of a dark horse, aincha, Pete?'

'OK. Cut the crap. It's gittin' late. I'd better go see where they are. Time to be headin' back.'

'Time for a tequila,' Estevan shouted. 'Time to celebrate, *amigo*. Murchison's been given a beating for the first time in his life.'

'Nope' – Pete watched Estevan pour the fiery liquid, lick at salt on the back of his hand, down it in one – 'I don't touch thet pizen any more. I'll jest take one more beer.'

Nathan leaned on the bar and scratched at his blond thatch. 'Say, if you need any hands I'd be proud to ride with you.'

'Aincha worried 'bout Comanches? We've jest lost five dead. Or repercussions from the Murchisons?'

'Nope. I reckon you can handle that, Pete.'

'Come on, then. I wanna hire some more men.'

They ambled out of the saloon, Estevan reluctantly abandoning the tequila bottle on Pete's instructions – he didn't allow liquor on the ranch – and strolled along to the corral.

Most of the men, who leaned on the rails watching the mustangs being busted, quietly shook their heads. They didn't want to know. They knew better than to go against the Murchisons.

Jim was sat on a post amid the swirls of dust, watching a wrangler hanging on to a cross-hobbled pony which he had managed to saddle, twisting his ear hard to hold him, while he swung aboard, letting him feel what it was like to have a man on his back, furiously quirting the bronc as it went bucking and bouncing away, hazing it with a rain slicker, staying in the saddle and finally riding it to a trembling bemused standstill.

Jim whooped with the rest of them. 'Ain't it exciting, Paw?'

'It ain't my way of breaking a horse,' Pete said. 'But I guess it's practical.'

A pony to most of these men was only a cheap work tool, which they rode until it was done, and then found another.

'You ain't having much luck with your recruiting,' Estevan laughed. 'These Texans are a yellow-livered bunch.'

'They ain't crazy,' Pete said, and looked across at the *vaqueros* who were watching the proceedings. There were three of them, a mean-eyed mob. And by their side a young fuzzy-haired black fellow, barefoot, skinny and in tatters, like he'd just escaped from some southern plantation. Two tame Indians, probably Apache scouts, one in a cavalry hat and baggy off-whites, the other in down-at-heel cowpuncher's clothes, a round-crowned hat, were crouched outside the cantina.

'Looks like I gotta take on the despised and

reviled ones,' Pete said, and they watched him amble over and begin haggling. One by one the men nodded, and followed him back.

'Waal, thet's settled. Let's go into the cantina and chow down. I'm famished. Could eat a grizzly bear. Jim, you go find your mother and bring her along.'

'You've been fighting,' Louisa said, when she joined them and saw the lump swelling up puffily around Pete's eye.

'You shoulda seen him Miz Bowen,' the new boy, Nathan cried. 'Wow! What a right! Never thought I'd see the day Hal Murchison went down.'

There was one more thing Pete had to do in town, so he excused himself, and went to find the undertaker and part-time lawman, Elijah Jones, to report his men dead. Elijah wasn't a bad fellow, but he had to stay the right side of the Murchisons.

'I heard what happened over at the saloon, Pete. You're playing with fire. Ain't a lot I can do to protect you if Abraham Murchison turns nasty.'

'Ain't him I'm worried about. It's the Comanch'. I want you to get an official letter through to San Antone, or maybe Judge Parker at Fort Smith, he's a friend of mine, although we're out of his jurisdiction here. I wanna know what them Yankee generals would say about providing some kinda reservation for the Comanch' if I could parley with Red Ant, get him to come down from the hills. Can they give a guarantee that him and his people will be treated right?'

Elijah rubbed his nose, got out his pen and began to make scratchy notes, splattering blobs of ink. 'This is a good idee. Let's git this right.

Somethun's gotta be done, thet's fer sure. Hundreds of settlers being slaughtered and run off their land. It's time they called the army in.'

'Sure, bring in the army,' Pete said. 'But, you're still goin' to need some peaceable solution in the end if the killin's gonna stop. Otherwise Red Ant will fight to his last man.'

'Mebbe I'll take this in person to San Antonio. Present it to the Governor, kinda like a petition. Let him know how we feel. Stage'll be goin' north tomorrow.'

'Sounds a good idea, Elijah. I'll leave it to you.'

The elderly lawman got to his feet and saw Pete to the door of his office. 'Aincha ever thought about becoming a Texas Ranger, Pete? If you were there'd be a lot of good men who would be ready to help you in trouble. The Murchisons would think twice about tangling with ya.'

'Ach.' Pete spat in the dust, quizzically. 'I've sure had enough of being lawman. Ain't got time, either. Spring round-up's coming. I'm planning to drive two thousand longhorns to Kansas.'

'They reckon Dodge City's the new place to go to.

'So mebbe that's where I'll go.'

SIX

A wild bunch they looked as they headed back across the plain to the Douro Canyon, the Mexicans riding their own horses, the Apaches and the black boy, Timothy, perched on the creaking wagon as Pete urged his team on. These men looked as if they might be on the run for one reason or another. Or, perhaps they were just natural wanderers. Out here it wasn't wise to enquire too closely about a man's history. If they could rope and ride, were ready to fight Comanche or rustler, that was all Pete asked. Timothy had never sat a horse or used a gun. Well, he would have to learn fast. If not, maybe he would make a good cook.

They travelled on through the night and it was dawn when they saw the Wild Rose ranch house. 'If it ain't the little grey filly,' Pete said. 'She's come in off the range. Looks like she don't want them Comanche to git her agin.'

'More like she remembers that corn you feed her in the winter and the warm stable,' Louisa laughed. 'She know where her bread has butter.'

'Remember how she ran off after you branded her, Pa?' Jim said. 'She must've forgiven ya.'

The filly was free to roam where she wished out

on the range, but in the past two winters Pete had brought her in to get her used to having a saddle put on her. She had kicked up a palaver at that, and bucked some more when it was off. She had packed the saddle for an hour or two each day, and gradually it got so she came when called, and didn't fight a bridle being put on her. She accepted the light snaffle bit and learned to turn, stop and go.

'I've a few more tricks to teach her. She may be one of the wild breed but she's smart as a whip and one of these days she's going to make a good cut horse,' Pete said.

'What's a cut horse, Pa?'

'I mean she will be able to feint and dodge and anticipate what a longhorn's liable to do and cut out the one we want from the herd. She's certainly fillin' out real strong. Reckon she's strong enough to carry you, Jim?'

'You mean, she's for me?'

'That's the idea.'

The boy jumped down and ran on ahead of the wagon. The grey shied away at first, but slowed, and allowed the boy to hug her neck, and lead her into the corral by her shaggy mane.

'Now look what you done,' Louisa said. 'I wanted him to get some sleep.'

'Aw, we can all have a siesta,' Pete said. 'Come on, Timothy, I gotta teach you a few things about hosses, too. First we better find you a pair of boots.'

They jumped down from the wagon and Matt ambled over to meet the new boys, unload the stores and show them their bunks. Pete got hold of one of the wisest old cow horses they had and took him along to the corral. That winter he had been trying to spook the filly, letting the saddle slip under her belly, which set her off kicking and bucking. Pete had let her play at the end of a long rope. When he figured the time was right he flipped the rope, landing the filly on her head. This had to be done on several occasions before the little grey learned not to kick up a fuss if the saddle slipped.

'Mebbe it looks like I'm being hard on her,' Pete told his son. 'But what if you were in the saddle and got your foot caught in the stirrup? You'd be kicked to bits.'

Pete had tried a few more tricks on her, tying an old cowhide to her neck, which made her stampede and bellow. But soon she would get a knowing look in her eye when he tried to spook her, as if to say, 'I know what you're trying' and go on eating her bran. Now he planned on putting her in a stall with the old horse, who, he was convinced, would put her straight on a few things. They had ways of communicating, and that was for sure.

Maybe it was being with the Comanche, or out on the range with the other mustangs, or being branded, but today the filly was acting feisty again, prancing around the corral. She was at the far end of the corral as if challenging them to catch her. Jim tried to lasso her but she dodged. 'What's the matter with her?' he cried.

'She's jest showing us we ain't goin' to have it all our own way. Now you watch this.' He spooked the filly out of the corner and threw a loop. The filly saw it coming and ducked. She looked mighty proud of herself and went to run on when she felt the rope around her front feet and before she knew it she was going head over heels.

Pete sat on her neck and held her down. 'That should teach her not to run across a spread rope,' he grinned. He put a hurry-up hackamore on her head and let her up. She stood trembling and snorting, but the fall had brought her to her senses and she was quiet after that, even when Jim got on her back.

The boy smiled, triumphantly, as he rode her slowly around. 'Gee, Pa, thanks. You're the best Pa in the world. And she's the most beautiful horse.'

'Now it's your turn, Timothy.' And he got him on the old cowhorse and showed him how to handle him.

At two o'clock Louisa clanged on an iron triangle and all the men went to sit at a long table under a canopy of cut branches and chowed down to enchiladas and beans. Looking at them Pete thought he might have the makings of an outfit.

He gave them all the afternoon free and, when Jim had gone to sleep, joined Louisa in their bed. For some unfathomed medical reason she had not had any more children after her first, unlike most settlers' wives. But it meant that, unlike most of them, she had kept the slim-waisted figure she had had as a girl, her body firm and full, soft as silk. They would both have liked to give Jim a brother or sister. As Pete took her in his arms he whispered, 'Mebbe we won't succeed, but we sure do have fun tryin'.'

SEVEN

How shallow was the great Rio Grande! The drought had reduced it to a ribbon of slow mud water. Pete and Estevan halted their horses at the water's edge in a grove of willows and looked up at the 1,500 feet walls of purple and red rock through which the river had zig-zagged. On the Texas side was the Mesa de Anguila (Plateau of Eels) and across the stream Mexico's Sierra Ponce. The canyon was a dark slit, and on their side, where the sun's rays reached, as hot as a bakehouse.

'Here we go,' Pete said, and kneed Nimrod across the river. 'It sure gonna be a steep climb. I'm a stranger in your country now.'

He had decided it would be too dangerous to cross the Muertos range – the hills were bristling with Comanche – and had opted for this deep and difficult detour to reach El Zapote's hideout. Estevan had agreed to lead them there.

On their mustangs behind him were Nathan, the two Apache scouts, and Miguel, one of the Mexicans, who had agreed to go on this sortie into the mountains, which would seem suicidal to most cowhands. It had to be done, that was all Pete knew, if his ranch was to be protected.

Turkey vultures and ravens floated lazily

watching them as they began their climb, almost as if they were hoping for a feed! In Indian file the small party zig-zagged for miles up the rugged slopes. It was a relief to men and animals to leave the desert scrub behind and move gradually into the cooler shade of other life zones, seeing new bird life appear among the piñon pines, chickadees and flycatchers singing and posturing.

And, as the afternoon drew on, and they had climbed some 6,000 feet, they entered yet another zone where strange trees of the northern Canadian forests, spruce and fir were preponderate. It was like climbing up into a giant island in the sky, and, as they approached the timberline, was beginning to get gloomy and cold.

They had seen no sign of other humans all day, except for an ancient wooden cross that had tumbled from a grave of stones. Who could it be? One of the *conquistadores*? Or a more recent Christian wanderer?

As darkness began to fall they made camp among the pines and soon had a small fire blazing, and roasted a peccary, or wild pig, they had shot in the canyon. 'Waal,' Nathan drawled, as he carved himself a slice, 'we sure ain't seen no sign of Injuns, 'cept for our friends here.'

The two Apache, or Tinneh – for Apache is only a Mexican word meaning enemy – sat watching, a look of disgust on their features. Pete remembered their feelings about the porcine tribe and offered them dried pony steaks, which they sniffed, suspiciously, but sank their teeth into. Far away in the distance, outlined blue against the night sky, were other mountain ranges, leading to the Chiricahua, their homeland, where

Cochise and his warriors roamed.

Pete had only a vague idea of what he was going to do when they found El Zapote, but he knew, and they knew, there was going to be shooting, and they did not say very much, but rolled up in their blankets, taking turns on guard.

The sinister hooting of screech owls through the night gave way to the more pleasant cooing of band-tailed pigeons at dawn, and the men roused themselves, clutched chilled hands around mugs of hot black coffee, and hit saddle leather again, crossing a ridge between two almost Alpine peaks, and plunging down a steep slope.

'They're over there,' Estevan said, pointing a leather-clad arm at a dark range – 'El Chisos, the Ghost Mountains. They hang out in an old silver mining town.'

'How long?' Pete said, squinting across the divide.

'Two, mebbe three days. It tough country.'

'They don't know we're coming so there ain't no hurry. Normally I believe in the strategy of the great generals, Napoleon Bonaparte and Stonewall Jackson, move fast, take 'em by surprise, and hit 'em hard, but I guess we gonna have to handle this kinda different. We ain't got enough firepower. You on reasonable terms with this El Zapote man?'

'Sure. I just hit the breeze, like I said. Got tired of their ways.'

'You reckon he might kinda be willing to take us on as hired guns?'

'Sure' – Estevan flashed his smile – 'why not?'

'Let's go then,' Pete cried. 'Hee-yaaaaagh!'

EIGHT

Crazy About Horses was not crazy about the way the sacred war against the whites was going. When he was a young man, he too had been a warrior, and had gone on the warpath against the horse-thieving Pawnees, and the Conchos, and even the fierce Apache to maintain the Comanche freedom to roam the vast plains without hindrance. Those had been the good days, when game was plentiful, before the wagons with white sails began to arrive bearing the terrible white people, who put up fences and foolish square houses, and claimed that the land was their own. The land had belonged to the Comanche forefathers since the world was born. Unlike the fawning Pawnees, Crazy About Horses had kept his tribe aloof from the white people, and had fought them bitterly whenever they appeared, narrowly missing death on many occasions; and he still had shrapnel in his leg from when one of their soldiers' cannons had killed his favourite horse. Once it had seemed that the Great Spirit had answered their prayers because the whites went off to slaughter each other in what they called the Civil War, although it didn't seem very civil to him. While they were busy fighting, the good days had returned. Crazy

About Horses had hoped they would devour themselves, but it was not to be. Again they had returned to claim Comanche lands and push them back up into these barren hills.

These were the thoughts that were passing through his mind as he sat cross-legged in the dust in the centre of the ragged teepees that was what his village had been reduced to. All the buffalo had gone and there were no hides left to repair the lodges, or to keep themselves warm in winter. As for food, he was getting tired of eating mesquite and rattlesnakes. His belly craved some buffalo hump. The whites had even rounded up the wild longhorn cattle that roamed the hills and claimed that they were theirs, and in the summer herded them all away to the north to load on to the iron horse. What they did with all those cattle he did not know. He only knew they shot at and sometimes killed any Comanche who tried to take one for himself and his starving family.

'These whites are unbelievable,' he muttered to the elders who sat in a silent circle waiting for his words. 'They do not understand that our hunting grounds are part of the Great Circle, that they must not be cut across by iron rails, that they belong to us.'

The elders shook their heads solemnly. There had been no great triumph when Red Ant's war party had returned, climbing their exhausted ponies up through the claw peaks of the Death Mountains. It was an apt name for there had been too many squaws widowed, too many children orphaned, and now Red Ant's brother had been killed in battle and by a small white boy.

'It is a strange omen that Black Cloud should

have been killed by a child,' one of them said. 'As if the Texans are saying, "Look, even our children can kill you".'

Instead of the drums beating out victory, there had been a good deal of wailing, self-immolation and frenzy as the dead warriors were mourned.

'I warned my son, Red Ant, not to go against the dark-haired man, Black Pit they call him. He is not like other hair-faces. He has offered us friendship and we refused him. They say that he helped the Kiowa of Kicking Bird's tribe when Custer tried to massacre them as they rode in to surrender at Bad Medicine Bluff. He lassoed and destroyed the gun that spits many bullets and helped them escape. He is a strange man possessed of guile and magic, a chief unto himself. He is subdued by no man. And now his son has killed my son. I think this could be a warning that we should cease our war against him.'

The women and children of the village had stopped their work and play, and sat about like wolves, watching the elders from a distance. They knew that some momentous decision was going to be made.

Red Ant stood by his lodge, naked but for a loin cloth and moccasins, his muscled body tense, his lance and fate-shield in his hand. He had returned without his brother's body and the people were trying to make him feel bad about that. They had not praised his brother's death as a glorious one. His band of warriors squatted around him, bows and war clubs in their hands, waiting for their commands. Many of their comrades had died, but they were willing to fight on, fight to the end. Wasn't that all they could do?

'Look at the old men,' one sneered. 'They have forgotten what it is to fight. How can they call themselves Comanches?'

Angrily, Red Ant strode over to the circle of elders, stood, defiantly, his feet astride, his arms folded, before them. His face was painted with red ant-like legs running from each side of his nose, and, similarly, around his ribs. About his head was the beaded band that held upon his forehead the Wheel of Fate made of red and white bristles, its inner circle of beads containing his sacred sign. It shielded the bridge of his nose. It defended him in battle. Two small luck feathers hung down across one ear, and the topknot of his hair was crowned by a flare of bristles like a bird's crest.

'We are ready to ride again,' he shouted. 'I will avenge my brother's death.'

'Why do you interrupt our council?' Crazy About Horses chided. 'Have you taken on the chieftainship of this tribe?'

'You sit here like old women,' Red Ant snapped. 'There is work to do. I need more of your horses to trade with the Mexicans for guns. We need rifles if the white man is to be driven from our lands.'

'Haven't I wasted enough of my ponies already? How many more must I give up?' Crazy About Horses said, miserably.

'You have enough. With rifles we will get you more.'

'And Black Cloud's widow? Are you going to take her into your lodge? And his children? Who is going to feed these mouths while you are away making war? What have you brought back for us? Only death.'

'I have brought the yellow coins from the box on

the coach we attacked, the gleaming beads from the people we killed. The Mexicans prize these. But we need horses, too, if they are to give us the guns.'

'Take them,' Crazy About Horses said, throwing up his hands. 'Go. Do what you must do. We will be waiting for you.'

Red Ant bounded over to the warriors. 'My father has finally come to his senses. He has given me horses to trade. No one can stop us now. I have news that El Zapote is coming. With rifles we will be invincible. We will ride down on to the plains like a scourge.'

The warriors began to howl and leap about, as a medicine man began a slow muffled beat on a skin drum to warn the whites that they were not defeated, that they were coming. The women watched, anxiously. They knew the meaning of this message. There would soon be more warriors to mourn.

NINE

When Pete's party reached lowland scrub, they turned east through a wilderness of eroded arroyos where ocotillos and creosote bushes struggled to survive, and great pyramids of rock reached into a harsh blue sky. The ragged band straggled on through the heat of this strange landscape, massive yuccas in creamy blossom, and hedgehog cactus clumped among the boulders, their flowers surrounded by murderous spines. Everything in this country seemed to bear thorns, hooks and needles, piercing the horses' legs, making going difficult, as if warning them of worse to come.

Towards evening, as they rode under an aproned butte, they saw the silhouette of several horsemen, silent, watching them on the skyline, and the whipcrack of a rifle shot rang out, barrelling and echoing against the canyon walls. Nimrod reared as a bullet chiselled rock near his hooves, and Pete swept his hat off and waved at the men.

'How many you make it?' he muttered. 'Eighteen?'

'Twenty, mebbe,' the blond youth, Nathan, replied. 'They sure got us dry-gulched. We ain't got a chance.'

'It's OK,' Estevan said, as another bullet whistled past. 'They ain't aiming to kill. Just make us dance.'

He shouted up to the men in Spanish, his words rippling and reverberating through the eroded chasms.

Soon, most of the men had disappeared from the height, and had galloped up to surround them, laughing and jeering at Estevan. 'You come back, eh?'

They were a fierce-looking band, their dark features hardened and eroded as the landscape, strung with bandoleers of bullets, dressed in tight leathers, or blanket coats, wearing wide sombreros. Yelping their harsh Castilian cries, they escorted the intruders up through a pass until they reached a collection of run-down adobe huts clustered about the entrance to a mine.

Pete's men, and their horses, thirstily eyed a small stream that trickled from the shaft, but first they had to talk. He dismounted with Estevan and was led into a long low hut, cornered with desert stone, holes in its adobe walls, its wattled mesquite roof sagging in near-collapse. A burly moustachioed Mexican sat at a table, a jug of liquor in one arm, a razor-thin Indian girl in the other. Piggy eyes in a squat, sweaty face were on them, and gold teeth flashed as he grinned. 'So, you didn't like *El Norte*, the Americanos?'

'Even your company is preferable,' Estevan said.

The big man laughed loudly, and squeezed the girl. 'He still the same big mouth, you see? He come back to me. He miss me. I treat him so good.'

Estevan doffed his hand at Pete. 'This is an *amigo* of mine. We done some rustling together but they run us off. I tell him it is easier down here to make a peso.'

'Yeah? You think so?'

'Sure. Pete, this is El Zapote. You surely heard of him?'

'Cain't say I have 'fore you mentioned him, but' – he proffered his gloved hand – 'pleased to make your acquaintance El Zapote, old bean.'

'Ha!' the Mexican roared, ignoring the out-stretched hand, refilling his glass. 'You like mescal?'

'Nope. I don't drink. My friend here does.'

'Estevan? Sure I know *he* does. What you do, mister?'

'I'm a soldier of fortune. Been in a little trouble up Kansas way. That's why I'm heading south of the border.'

'Ha! What kinda trouble? Why you don' drink with El Zapote?'

'Like to keep my trigger finger steady. You got a beer I gladly drink with ya.'

'Trigger finger? You reckon you shoot?'

With eased skill one of Pete's .44s was in his hand and pointing at El Zapote's chest. He slowly cocked it. A glint in his eye made the bandit chief swallow. Maybe he had been sent to kill him? Pete half-smiled and whispered, 'You see them nails in thet pole along the end there. Looks to me like they oughta be hammered home.'

He spun around, the .44 roared, and, when the smoke cleared, six bullets had hit the nail heads driving them in deep. As some of his gun-runners crowded in El Zapote whistled. 'Jesu Maria, the

Americano shoot good. It OK. He jest showin' me. You wanna work for me, gringo?'

'That's the general idea,' Pete said, twirling his gun, stuffing it back into its greased holster. 'When do we start?'

'When I give the orders. You have fun here. We got girls. We got music. We even got beer. You and your boys relax. Tomorrow, maybe, we get goin'. We even got a little entertainment.'

Estevan looked up, sharply. He knew his ex-leader's taste in sadism. 'Who might that be?'

'Julio. You remember Julio? He thought he could sell us to the Federales. He didn't know that I had already bought 'em.' Again El Zapote roared with laughter, thrust his hand into the woman's blouse. 'It so happens I could do with some more men. You're hired, gringo. Now you go.'

As Pete stepped out of the doorway, El Zapote pulled his revolver from his belt and blew his hat off.

'I can shoot, too, *comprende*? Remember, gringo, it don't do to doublecross El Zapote.'

Pete, who had frozen, bent down to pick up his hat. He looked back and smiled. 'I'll bear that in mind.'

TEN

The strains of guitar and marimba starting up after sundown attracted Pete and his party over to the long adobe hut. Most of the *bandidos* were stood around passing a liquor jar of mescal, smoking vile smelling *cigarillos* of some local weed, and were already pretty high (spirited that is). Two of them had grabbed hold of Mexican wenches and were stamping their boots doing some kind of fandango as the girls whirled their frilled skirts displaying shapely brown legs, giving wild shrieks. Two other girls were lying on a palliasse on the floor being fondled immodestly by four outlaws. El Zapote sat in state at his table and chair, his lithe and impassive Indian queen on his knee, watching the frolics with a wise smile.

'Aieee, *hombre!*' he shouted, beckoning Pete over with his knife. 'How you like my entertainment? You want one of my girls, you have one. You are welcome to my humble abode.'

'Thanks,' Pete said. 'Where 'n hell did you find 'em in this desert? There ain't a town in a hundred miles.'

'I stole them from a brothel in Guiadado. The music men, too. They real good, eh?'

Pete looked over at the bald and corpulent marimba player flicking his hammers dexterously over his instrument, a look of sad despair on his face. 'Sure are. *He* looks kinda homesick, though.'

'Sure, he will get used to our little ways. So will you.'

There wasn't much in the way of furniture in the place, apart from some wooden burro saddles, so Pete sat himself down on one, and stretched out his long legs. 'Aw, hail, we might as well enjoy ourselves,' he said, as Nathan offered him a wooden beaker of watery white fluid.

'Good, good.' El Zapote beckoned. 'You drink. Beer made from mesquite.'

'Don't look much different to mescal,' Pete muttered, but he screwed up his eyes and took a good swig.

There were loud cries from outside and hoisted through the door was a wagon wheel, with underneath it, his arms tied to the spokes, a man, who they guessed must be Julio. He tottered, his face bloodied, his legs weak, as they howled and pushed him back and forth. Into the broken wall a wagon axle had been fixed, and willing hands hoisted the wheel up to fix it on the wall, Julio vainly kicking, until his ankles, too, were tied.

A thunder of explosions rattled the loose rafters as the Mexicans, grinning and laughing, pulled their revolvers and blasted away at poor Julio, using him for target practice. Not unnaturally, a look of terror transfixed his features as he was slowly spun. He shrieked as a bullet shattered his forearm and blood and bone splattered the wall.

El Zapote roared a warning. He didn't want him to die too fast. In the fug of gunpowder smoke, dust and dislodged debris, the six *compadres* from Wild Rose ranch watched uneasily. There was little they could do but pretend to enjoy the horseplay. A Mexican was chalking numbers up around the wheel and set to spinning Julio again. He was to be a living, or half-living roulette wheel. The bandits found this hilarious, throwing coins down, shouting their bets.

When they had had enough, El Zapote lurched over to the man, slashed his knife across his face, cut strips of flesh from his ribs, tore them upwards, began to hack at his ears, his nose, and other more intimate protruberances. Not unnaturally Julio screamed horribly. El Zapote drooled over him and finished him with a twist into the heart. Blood gouted.

The room had fallen silent, the girls and the musicians staring in horror, even the *bandidos* subdued. El Zapote turned to his new guests, with his crooked smile, wiping his knife on his bloodied shirt, and croaked, 'Now, hombres, it's your turn.'

Black Pete made a move for his holsters, but it was too late. He and his men looked up into the deathly holes of some twenty revolvers pointed at them. They could die now, or surrender their arms, and maybe go the slow way.

'So, you are not so fast as El Zapote? Drop your gunbelts, slowly, *amigos*. That's right. Now who is going to talk? Maybe the kid? Put him on the wheel.

Pete went to protest as they caught Nathan, but a boot caught him, sickeningly, in the gut, a revolver butt slammed down on the back of his neck, and the fists of two other men smashed into his face. He slumped back to the floor. Again there was nothing he could do but watch.

Watch as Nathan, with his bristly blond country-boy thatch, his blue eyes like marbles, kicking and struggling, half-strangled, was hoisted up, roped to the wheel, put in motion, and the shooting match began. Pete winced as he saw one bullet crease a red parting across the young cowboy's scalp. He liked this kid.

The smoke drifted away as the yelling of the firing-squad ceased, and they flicked spent cases from hot cylinders, and began to reload. El Zapote approached Nathan and slashed his knife across his shirt, leaving a thin trickle of blood.

'You tell us, kid, where you come from? Who is this man Pete? What you want here? Or you get the same as Julio.' He thumped Nathan's chest and roared with laughter. 'Believe me, El Zapote he enjoy cutting you up.'

Nathan's face was pale and strained, his lips pursed. He was tied, helplessly, but his voice was clear and full of contempt as he spoke. 'If you ain't never heard of Pete Johnson, one of the Johnson boys, you ain't never heard of nobody.'

'Johnsons?' El Zapote muttered, seeming to remember something. 'Who are the Johnsons?'

'Jesus, you sure are dumb. They're one of the most notorious outfits in Missouri. Rode with the Quantrill Raiders, robbed banks and trains with Jesse and Frank James. That man's one of the most notorious outlaws in America. That's all I know about him.'

'Yeah?' El Zapote leered. 'You talk shee-it. You want more treatment? Here.' And he spun the wheel again, backing away, pulling his six-gun, a signal for more noisy roulette. The odds against young Nathan staying unscathed, or alive, were fast shortening.

'Now what you say?' El Zapote asked, as he called another halt, his face up close to Nathan's.

Nathan spat in his eye. 'You fat pig. Do what you like. I tell you, you're going to live to regret it if the Johnson clan finds out. He's got a price on his head.'

El Zapote wiped the spittle out of his eye, and turned to Pete. 'Is that true, *hombre*?'

Pete shrugged and nodded. 'Kid didn't oughter go blabbing his mouth like that.'

'What about you?' El Zapote shrieked, grabbing hold of Miguel's rough blanket overcoat. 'How you meet him?'

Miguel stared stonily back and said in Spanish. 'North of the border. Broken Bow. We rustled the Murchisons' herd. Posse came after us.'

El Zapote released him, looked at Estevan, and burst into hysterical laughter. 'Cut him down,' he cried, thrusting his revolver in his belt. 'I forgive him for spitting in my eye.'

The guitarist and the marimba man began hesitantly to play again; the frozen-faced girls relaxed, Nathan regained the ground, spun on his legs dizzily, and landed on the seat of his pants. El Zapote emptied his jug of liquor over his head. Nathan howled at the searing crease in his scalp.

'That will kill the maggots, *amigo*,' El Zapote said, and hoisted him up.

Nathan's eyes bulged, but he gritted his teeth, grabbed one of the girls, and swung her around in a dance of relief that he was still alive.

El Zapote offered a jug to Pete. 'You understand, gringo, I got to be careful. I can trust no one. Everybody try kill me.'

'Sure,' Pete drawled, wiping the blood from his face, accepting the jug, taking a tentative swig. 'Why not? I know the feeling.'

'You OK. I trust you. I pay you well, you see.'

'What exactly do the Comanche give you for the guns?'

'Sometimes rustled cattle, sometimes horses.'

So, that's what's been happening to my stock, he thought.

'One time they had silver nuggets and many ornaments and pelts, but we cleaned them out of them. Sometimes they trade us their widowed squaws. They fetch a good price as slaves in the mines, or the bordellos.'

'I'd prefer to be paid in gold.'

'So would I, *señor*,' El Zapote roared. 'The Comanche are getting wise to that. When they raid the *ranchos* they see if there is anything about before burning them down. Maybe Red Ant has gold. I hear he has been busy.'

'Red Ant? Who's he?'

'The Comanche warrior we trade with. Tomorrow we will go.'

And he slapped Pete's shoulder, staggered back to his table, scooping Nathan up on the way.

Pete had not been offered his gunbelt back, but he could see where it lay. 'Let 'em git drunk,' he muttered to his men. 'We better bide our time.'

He wasn't sure how far he could rely on Miguel and the Apaches if it came to a fight. Or Estevan, either. He had a bottle in his hand and was getting riotously drunk with his old Comanchero pals. They might decide they preferred to work for El Zapote to being hard-ridden cowhands.

The greasy chieftain had taken some kind of fancy to Nathan, and, as the evening festivites whirled on, he engaged him in a noisy bout of arm-wrestling. Nathan's youthful build was no match for Zapote's bear shoulders. But, he gave a grin, and a slight wink at Pete, as he put his right hand up for another try. As their fingers clasped, Nathan's left hand slipped El Zapote's revolver from his belt and he put it to the Mexican's head. El Zapote had time to give only a gasp of surprise before his brains were spluttered out over the Indian girl.

Pete rolled across the floor, whipped out his Smith and Wessons from their holsters and it was like an inferno as he fired off a dozen shots. The Mexicans spun like rag dolls. The two Apaches ran in blazing their carbines. Miguel and Estevan snatched up revolvers and fired point blank at the men they had been drinking with.

The battle lasted only a few minutes. There was a sudden silence, punctuated by moans and screams. As the gunsmoke drifted away a frieze of bloody bodies were revealed lolled on the floor, on top of each other, or against the walls. All the Comancheros had been accounted for except for a wounded one who was raising his revolver. Estevan blasted him into extinction.

'See if you can git them two guards,' Black Pete said to the Apaches. 'There's one on each side of the pass. We'll have a look around to see if there ain't no more skulking around.'

One of the dancehall girls had caught a bullet in her chest. 'Too bad,' Estevan said, as he kneeled down to close her eyes. 'I fancied this one.'

'At least we didn't shoot the marimba man,'

Nathan said. 'C'mon, start with the music. We don't want to make them guards suspicious.'

The youth strode over and stared down at El Zapote's decapitated crown. 'I owed him that,' he said.

ELEVEN

'We done a good job and cleaned out a nest of rattlesnakes,' – in the morning sunshine Pete was watching his men haul the corpses out and load them on the mules – 'help yourselves to whatever you can find on 'em. By way of bonus. Don't overload yourselves. We got some hard ridin' to do. Maybe more fighting yet.'

'I shoulda asked El Zapote where he kept his loot before I dispatched him to hell,' Nathan said. 'It must be in a cave around here somewhere.'

'There will be much gold and silver,' Miguel muttered. 'He was a greedy, crafty one. It will be hidden.'

'What we waiting for?' Estevan pitched in. 'Let's go search for it.'

Pete didn't think it worth his while arguing. Once a man had got gold fever there wasn't much you could do except wait until it wore off. 'You do what you durn well please today. Only first we gonna toss these critters over the precipice. They beginning to stink the place up. Tomorrow we ride out.'

'Hang on,' Estevan said. 'If we going to meet the Comanche we gotta look like Comancheros. How about you put on their clothes?'

'Thet ain't a bad idea,' Pete agreed, picking up a wide sombrero and trying it for size. 'How do I look? El Zapote sure ruined my hat.'

'Aw,' Nathan moaned. 'It's taken me two years to get the right creases in my stetson. I ain't givin' it up. I don't wanna look like no durned greaser. No offence, Miguel.'

'You better do like Estevan says if you wanna keep your scalp.'

'What we gonna do with these gals and the orchestra?'

'Don't rightly know,' Pete said, and began to parley in Spanish with a woman called Mercedes, who was dark and muscular and seemed to be their natural leader. She grinned her gold teeth at him, and kicked El Zapote in his gut. 'I hate the pig. I glad you kill him,' she shouted.

Mercedes consulted with the five other girls and the 'orchestra' and Pete explained to Nathan, 'They seem scared to go overland a hundred miles back home in case they run into more of El Zapote's men. They wanna come with us. I've told 'em to put the *bandidos* clothes on, too. Even if they cain't sling a gun it will help make a show.'

The girls were screaming and laughing, hauling the tight embroidered pants off the bandits, pulling their own dresses off, putting on shirts and bandoleers of bullets, hobbling around in boots that were too big for them, and sombreros. They seemed happy because for once in their lives they were the equals of men, not their slaves.

'Don't see why you shouldn't become citizens of the newly United States,' Pete told them, grinning at their antics. He wasn't sure the Comanches were going to be fooled, but it was worth a try.

'There's a town called Broken Bow. I reckon you can make a living there in your particular entertainment line.'

'How about you?' he asked the Indian woman, who was watching, her aquiline features grave, her hair hanging down to her waist. 'You going back to your people? Or you wanna come fight the Comanche?'

For answer, she slipped off her ragged dress, standing naked before them, and said, 'I come with you.'

'Whoowhee!' Nathan whistled, scratching at the soft golden stubble on his chin. 'She can be my *compadre* any day.'

He picked her up, and, with a wild war whoop, carried her away up the hill. At that Miguel and Estevan, and even the Apaches, began grabbing at the girls, who didn't seem at all eager to repel their advances, but began cracking bullwhips, and shooting off six-guns, and, laughing and shrieking, herded the men back into the tumbledown houses.'

Pete shrugged, bemused by the spectacle. 'Looks like we're goin' to have a party,' he said to the musicians. 'You boys better go in and get things swinging. Guess I gotta do the dirty work.'

He began heaving the half-naked Mexican corpses back on to the mules and it took him most of the morning before he had them pitched over the cliff. The sounds of merriment were still going on, so he went to explore the big mine shaft. There was a pile of Springfield rifles and ammunition waiting to be shifted out. It gave Pete an idea, and he pulled out his knife and began tampering with the rifles and sorting through the boxes of bullets.

It was gone three by the time he had finished that, and inspected the other stores. Among them was a case of bottles of castor oil, and two cases of whiskey. It gave him another idea. He began emptying most of the whiskey from the bottles and refilling them with castor oil.

The camp had gone quiet. Only the chubby Mexican gal, Maria, was crouched by the fire, dressed in a pair of tight *vaquero's* trousers, her large breasts bare and lolling, a sombrero on her head. She was poking at the flames to boil up a tin bath of water.

'Where is everybody?' he said.

'They gone look for treasure. You wan I give you nice bath, Mistuh Pete?'

'Waal, I sure could so with one after handling them durn stiffs,' he drawled. 'Guess I'm due a little rest and recreation, myself.'

Maria soon had the water warm, and Pete sighed, as he lowered himself in it and she leaned over, her big-nippled breasts bobbing in the water, and began to gently soap him, her fingers exploring all kinda places they didn't ought to do. This *señorita* sure seemed mighty grateful to her liberators. Pete lay back and lit a cheroot and closed his eyes. He didn't want to put himself anywhere where El Zapote might have been, nor be unfaithful to Louisa again. But, he guessed if he thought about her hard there wouldn't be any harm done, and Maria's lithe-fingered massage sure was mighty soothing. He put out a hand and cupped her breasts as she worked, pretending they were Louisa's. He wondered, with a tinge of guilt, how she was coping.... 'Oh, Jesus! That's nice,' he groaned. 'Do it some more.'

*   *   *

A hot day dawned, temperature over 100°, and, at
breakfast, as Pete looked at his small band – five
whores, two musicians, the squaw, two tame
Apaches, Nathan, Miguel and Estevan, he muttered, 'Guess I bin in better armies.' He thought of
the Cherokee cavalry he had led, and of Robert E.
Lee and his squirrel shooters, who had given the
northern blue-belly forces many a lesson in wild
courage. But even they had been defeated by
superior numbers. Up in those mountains, Los
Muertos, there would be about two or three hundred Comanche warriors on the prowl.

'I reckon it's time to give you some target
practice,' he growled, tossed the coffee out of his tin
cup into the ashes, and went to set up some castor
oil bottles.

'Right,' he said, handing Mercedes a .45. 'Start
shooting.'

The explosions echoed away through the mountain chasms. The bottles were still standing. Mercedes swore in lurid Spanish.

'You gotta take account of the kick,' he sighed.
'Aim lower. Try holding it in two hands. It's a durn
heavy gun. Git a glove on your left hand. Grip the
cylinder hard. Once you've shot your rounds be
ready to eject the empty cases and reload. Do it
quickly, but calmly. If you panic you're dead.
That's the way. Now try again.'

Mercedes whooped as this time one of the bottles
went flying. 'That's better,' Pete said, and stood
behind Maria, steadying her hand. 'This is a .36
cap and ball Remington, more of a lady's gun. You
can do it. Go on. Squeeze, don't jerk the trigger.'

Again the explosions crashed out, and again the bottles stood unscathed. 'Mebbbe you'd do better with a rifle. Try this Springfield. Come on, who's next?'

Estevan and Miguel set to showing the girls how to load and fire, and Pete shook his head, sadly, as bullets ricocheted in all directions. There were squeals of delight when one of the girls smashed a bottle. The musicians weren't a lot better, either.

'OK, hold it,' Pete shouted, after ten minutes of noisy pandemonium. 'You seem to have got the general idea. Cain't see you improving much before we meet the Comanch'. Being gunmen jest ain't your vocation, I guess.'

In frustration, he spun around, whipping out his Smith and Wesson, firing at six bottles he had set up, their open nozzles facing him, twenty paces away. Each of his bullets entered the neck exploding the glass.

'Hey!' Nathan shouted. 'It's me you should be giving lessons to.'

'My right-hand gun's for fanning.' Pete showed him the weapon with its seven and a half inch barrel. 'See the hammer? Filed down smooth. You hit it with your left palm, swing round, maybe you can get three or four men that way in one sweep, You gotta know what you're doin'. Takes a delicate touch.'

He broke the revolver, clearing the frame, and all the spent cartridges flew out simultaneously. 'That's another difference to the Colt. Saves a few seconds if you're in a hurry to reload. And in this country you generally are. Try it.'

Nathan tried it, pursing his lips with concentration, drawing, swinging around, smashing three of the bottles in the row, but fumbling slightly, his fingers splayed.

'Good. You've got a precise eye. Practise every day, Nathan, you'll soon be real fast.'

'This cylinder's getting damn hot,' Nathan said, handing the weapon back. 'You ever meet any of the famous lead slingers? Jesse James uses this kinda shootin' iron, don't he?'

'He weren't partic'lar fast. Neither him, nor Cole. They were jest murderous bastards who loved killing. Still do, I hear. They kill unexpectedly and without reason, put fear into people, even their own men. Not that I ever had a run-in with 'em. We were on the same side after all.'

Estevan laughed. 'You don't idolize them like the great American public do?'

'Most of the criminals I've tangled with have been cowards at heart. Like that Blue Jay Rogan I went after for the bounty two years ago. Full of nasty tricks. A renowned back-shooter. I sure wasn't sorry to see him hang.'

'Ain't you got any heroes?' Nathan asked.

'Well, one man I did have respect for was thet brigadier general, Kit Carson. A fine frontierman. Cain't say I much liked his ruthless burnt-earth campaign against the Navajoes, but he sure knew how to shoot. He always said – and you all should remember this – take your time. Never try to be faster than you are. Be in control. Draw, aim, fire. One fluid motion. And he said you should let your opponent feel you've got this power, that you can kill him. Kinda give him the last rites before you draw. Mebbe then you won't have to.'

As they turned away a thin pink snake, five feet long, slithered out of a pile of rocks, disturbed by the explosions. It stood its ground in front of them, its triangular head held high on its neck, weaving slowly.

'Durn me, I ain't never seen one like that,' Nathan said, as Pete stayed his gun hand. 'Wouldn't like him slidin' 'cross my pillow.'

'It's a red racer,' Pete said. 'Gutsy li'l critter. A gunman can learn a lot by watching the way he moves, not backin' off, occupying his own space; alert and ready to attack like streaked lightning; take the battle to the enemy. Red Ant's got one of them as a pet. That's the kind of man we're huntin'.'

They all laughed, nervously, as the snake decided he had made their acquaintance and slid off on his way.

It was an odd assortment of Comancheros who moved off later in the day with their string of burros. Gradually they climbed through the Joshua trees and fantastically-shaped cactii and rocks of the painted desert, and up into the hills again. But this time they were headed for the grim, grey, eroded fortress of Los Muertos.

Nonetheless, they were a merry band, the Mexican guitarist playing as he rode, the girls chattering like parrots, Estevan serenading them, and even the sore crease on Nathan's scalp could not quell his youthful exuberance. The Indian woman, now that she was free of El Zapote's embraces, smiled radiantly. She was one of the Concho tribe and he had captured her from her village away towards Chihuahua. She seemed to have taken a fancy to Nathan. Pete thought maybe Louisa could find her a job on the ranch, if they pulled through in one piece.

On the second day they descended to a lava desert, its flows eroded into weird forms over millions of years by The Great Sculptor. As dust devils swirled across the flats the sense of space awed them into silence and all that could be heard was the creak of harness and the breathing of the animals. They passed through tall saguaros, cylindrical cactii with crowns of creamy flowers. And slowly climbed up into the mountains to which the Comanches had retreated.

'You reckon you on the right route for the rendezvous?' Pete asked, as they dismounted that night and looked out across the purple ranges of hills set like dark cut-outs against the twilight sky.

'Reckon so,' Estevan said, scratching his curly mop, and pointing to a spiral of smoke rising from one of the higher hills some miles ahead. 'And I reckon they know we are here.'

'We'll camp here and put out double watch.'

TWELVE

The lone Comanche rode his horse slowly towards them across the plateau of the mesa, kicking up puffs of dust, coming out of apparent emptiness, but Pete knew they were being watched from the rim of rocks behind. The Comanche held a wand of feathers in his hand signifying peace, and rode bareback, without a bridle, a single feather in his long black hair. He paused a few paces in front of Estevan, who was riding point.

Pete sat his black stallion further back, in his colourful poncho, and sombrero, his bandanna covering his face in case they had met before. He had advised the girls to do likewise, and they were fanned out among the men. With luck the brave might get the idea they were El Zapote's men.

The brave had a buckskin sack in his other hand and he threw this to Estevan. It contained jewellery and gold coins obviously stolen from white people. He made the sign for cattle and horses and pointed back to the rim rocks. Estevan went to the *burros*, broke open a box and produced a Springfield single shot rifle. He took a .45 calibre bullet from his belt, inserted it, cocked the sidehammer, and aimed at a rock. The crack echoed across the plateau, and a whiff of black smoke hung in the air. Estevan went to another *burro* and took from its canvas bag a box of .45 slugs. He inserted one in the Springfield and threw the rifle and bullets to the Indian.

The Comanche examined it, curiously, and fired off a shot in the air. Estevan pulled forward another mule, put his hand in its sack and brought out a bottle of liquor, or what passed for it. He offered the brave a swig. The Indian took a sup, made a sour face, and let out a yell of joy. He stuck his peace wand into the ground and went racing back to the ridge, a rifle in one hand, bottle in the other.

'There's more castor oil than liquor in that bottle,' Pete said. 'It's a lowdown white man's trick, I know, but all's fair as they say, in love and war.'

They heard a whooping and a pack of Comanches on horseback came riding over the rim, and slowly down towards them, driving a herd of about a hundred longhorns, bellowing and braying, and a gaggle of ponies, charging in a plume of dust. Nathan and Miguel rode to intercept the herd and bring them to a halt, and Estevan handed the *burros* and their packs over to the Comanches. Pete and his 'boys' stayed back, their hands on their guns, and watched the Indians snatch at the *burros'* ropes and go charging away.

There was no sign of Red Ant, but Pete guessed he was watching from the rim. He rarely let a white man get the chance of an easy shot at him. He just don't trust us, Pete thought. And I don't blame him.

As the Comanche disappeared over the hill Pete

looked at the brand. They were Wild Rose, all right. 'Kinda ironic, ain't it,' he said. 'Gittin' paid in my own stock?'

'What now?' Estevan asked.

'Give 'em an hour and we'll follow. Ought to catch them Comanche with their pants down.'

Pete examined the bangles and bracelets, and the gold coin in the buckskin bag. 'Boys, if my guess is right, this ain't rightly our'n. I'm gonna have to hand it in to the sheriff at Broken Bow. I reckon it's what was stole offen the passengers that were massacred in the attack on the stage a while back.'

'Who'n hell's gonna know that?' Nathan said.

'Boy, I'm gonna know it. I was a lawman once, and I got a family. I gotta set an example and be honest. Them Comanch' must be desperate short of ammo if they're willin' to give these rings and things away.'

He saw the girls and the men watching him, envy in their eyes. They were getting greedy. They had already robbed the Comancheros and hadn't done too badly, although they hadn't found El Zapote's treasure. Most of them hadn't had two bits to their name before they met Pete. On the other hand they might all well be dead within another hour.

'Aw, hell,' he muttered. 'Ain't no good to them stage passengers. You can have it as a ree-ward. To the victor the spoils, like they say. Let's hope you hang on to your scalps long enough to enjoy it.'

'You are not going after them,' Maria protested, in shrill Spanish. 'You must be *loco*.'

'Ah reckon mebbe thet's so,' Pete said, sticking a boot-toe into his bentwood stirrup and hoisting himself into the saddle. 'C'mon, *muchachas*, let's ride.'

And, leaving two of the girls and the marimba player to herd the cattle, they set off at a fast lope in the direction the Comanche had gone.

The Indians must have got stuck into the castor oil straight away, for there's nothing a brave covets more than white man's liquor. And although the Caucasian was mainly to blame for the slaughter of the buffalo that was currently in full swing, the Aborigine did his fair share of wanton killing simply to swap buffalo tongues for a bottle of whisky. Neither side were innocent. And if the Indian hadn't helped the white man to shoot his redskin brother maybe this war on the frontier might have reached another conclusion.

Be that was as maybe; one thing was for sure, the savage certainly had an appetite for anything in a bottle. It was certainly not difficult to follow this trail. They could almost do so by the number of discarded whiskey bottles. And pretty soon they started seeing signs that Red Ant's boys were having difficulty controlling their bowel movements.

As they came over a brow of that wild and desolate plateau they saw a strange sight, nearly twenty of the Indians squatted among the rocks, their leggings and breech clouts down around their ankles, moaning and holding their guts and desperately voiding themselves. And a similar number who watched from horseback looked kind of queasy. Some were still tipping bottle to their mouths and hoping, vainly, for some mind expansion.

Red Ant had pleaded with the warriors to behave themselves, and to get the cargo of guns back to their village, but it had fallen on deaf ears. Once an Indian thought he was going to get the almost religious ecstasy, to him, of drunken obliteration, all other aims were forgotten.

'Hit 'em hard, *muchachas*,' Black Pete yelled, and led the charge down the hillside firing his Winchester repeating rifle from the shoulder, toppling from their saddles warriors grouped around Red Ant, leaving the ones squatted in the rocks to be rounded up by the girls and the Apaches.

The Mexicans, Miguel, and Estevan, who had once nearly lost his curly hair to this bunch, rode in close beside him, firing their revolvers to telling effect. Red Ant, vicious surprise on his handsome face, tried to fire his new Springfield in retaliation, but it appeared to jam, or not fire, as did those of his other braves. He did not realize that Black Pete had tampered with the mechanisms, and ruined most of the bullets. But now he saw him and recognized him, this tall man on his big black stallion bearing down upon him, and he gave a howl of vengeance, pulled his scalping knife, spun his pony, and leaped on Pete's back as he passed. They both went rolling onto the rock.

Estevan, Nathan, and Miguel had turned their horses to make another charge, the crash of their six-shooters making blood flower on copper skins, and to send once-proud braves toppling into the dust. It was a wipe-out. The surprised Indians had little chance; the expert aim of the three

gunmen and their heavier firepower cut them
down.

When Miguel had emptied both his revolvers he
pulled a machete from under his long blanket coat
and, on horseback, furiously fought a Comanche
with a stone war club. There was a clash of steel
on stone and the club was broken in half. Miguel's
backward thrust slashed through the brave's
jugular.

Nathan was wrestling another Indian who was
after his blond scalp, and the Apaches were busy
taking scalps for themselves. The bordello girls,
firing off their .45's wildly, were proving more
dangerous to their own side.

Down in the dust Pete was scrabbling with Red
Ant, whose strongly-muscled arm was bringing
his knifepoint closer and closer to his face, his
savage coutenance a retch of hatred. Pete
managed to scramble clear, dragging out his own
bowie knife.

The two leaders, the last of the combatants on
the field, circled each other like scorpions, making
feints and darts at each other with their
razor-honed weapons. Pete's *muchachas* stood
and watched, wondering whether to make bets on
the outcome. Suddenly Red Ant gave a howl and
leapt in, his knife aimed at Pete's heart, missing
by a fraction as the young rancher moved aside
and viced the Comanche's knife-arm under his
own, bringing his left hand up to twist back the
Indian's wrist, breaking the knife from his hold,
at the same time swinging him to his knees.
Before Red Ant could recover Pete smashed his
left fist into his jaw, and the side of his knife-hand
slammed into his ear, and, before he knew it, the

cowboy was on top of him, his knee in his back pinning him to the rock. His bowie was pressing into his feathered temple.

'Take his scalp,' one of the Apache urged. 'You have victory.'

Red Ant gave a sob of humiliation as his arms were twisted behind him, and he looked around at his decimated war party and awaited execution. He looked up at the skies and howled his disappointment at the gods.

'Gimme that lariat,' Pete growled. 'Me and Red Ant's goin' someplace.'

Estevan tossed a rawhide rope to him and he snaked it around Red Ant's neck and securely bound his wrists behind him.

The Apaches wanted to massacre and scalp the prisoners, according to their custom, but Pete stopped them. The Comanche braves didn't look very brave, in fact, looked mighty sorry for themselves as they took a tongue-lashing from Red Ant. 'Tie 'em up,' Pete said. 'A man can have enough of killing.'

'Looks like the operation was a success, *amigo*,' Estevan grinned. 'El Zapote's vipers cleaned out; a victory over the Indians and the capture of one of their most notorious warriors. All thanks to castor oil. That was a great idea of yours.'

'Don't be too cock-a-hoop,' Pete said. 'We got a tidy pace to go. We still in hostil' country.' But, he, too, felt relieved, as he smiled and said, 'Anybody got a cigarette?'

THIRTEEN

Even in bonds Red Ant had a natural grace about him as he rode his pony, his head held proudly, the strange 'bird of paradise' head-dress his only decoration, apart from warpaint. His wrists were tied behind him and Pete led him by a noose around his neck. With whoops and wuhays his *muchachas* ambled the cattle and horses and their prisoners behind them. It was easy enough to follow the trail that would guide them to the Comanche camp.

Maria had said he was crazy to go on, but he had replied that he certainly wasn't trailing the herd all the way back through the mountains the way they had come. 'We gotta sort out the rest of these buzzards before we head home,' he told her.

She had ridden up alongside him now, her breasts pushing and her large backside bouncing in the tight Comanchero outfit she had on. 'Mistuh Pete,' she grinned. 'When we get to your ranch I give you another bath.'

'You sure won't. And you keep mum, or my wife will tear you apart. Might see you in Broken Bow sometime. That's if we get out of this alive.'

They camped that night, and early morning brought them to the canyon leading into the

Comanche village. The first he knew of it was an arrow that hissed past his ear and lodged in Maria's rump. With a yelp of pain she leapt from the saddle and tried to pull the arrow out.

'Don't break it off,' Pete warned her, hanging tight to Red Ant, whipping out his .44 and looking around for whoever was on the hilltop. But the guard had sprinted off to rouse the camp.

Estevan had jumped down and was carefully pulling the arrow out of Maria. He ripped her pants away, put his mouth to the wound, and sucked at the blood in case the arrow had been poisoned, spitting it out.

'You bunch stay here and take cover,' Pete gritted out. 'Me and Red Ant's going on ahead.'

As they did so, with howls and screams to rouse their courage, the old men, led by Crazy About Horses, the young boys, and the few warriors who had not gone with the war party, ran to the entrance to their village and, as they saw Red Ant in ropes, stopped in their tracks, brandishing lances, war clubs and bows.

Pete eyed them, the remnants of another, possibly better, race. But, remnants they were. They had outlived their Time. He kept Red Ant close and put his rifle to the back of his head.

Crazy About Horses raised his arms to silence his warriors. He had not had time to put on his war bonnet or his buckskin shirt, and his body was withered and sagging, his hair hanging loose and grey-streaked, his face rumpled.

'Don't fire,' he shouted. 'I cannot lose two sons.'

The women and children were climbing up on to the rocks on either side, slings and stones in their hands, but they, too, paused like statues. Only one small boy hurled his rock and it landed at the hooves of Black Pete's stallion.

He smiled at the childish effort and nudged Red Ant forward.

'My son, what has happened to your comrades?'

'Many are dead.'

'It is Black Pit,' the chieftain exclaimed, puckering up his eyes and recognizing the young rancher. 'I warned you this man is a magic warrior.'

'It wasn't magic, father,' Red Ant replied, sullenly. 'He tricked us. He pretended to be a Comanchero and sold us guns that did not shoot, and whiskey that made my men sick. They had to keep running into the rocks to squat. How could they fight like that?'

'You fool. I warned you how clever he is.'

'Kill him, father,' Red Ant hissed. 'Go on. Kill him now. I don't care if he kills me. If we surrender I have nothing left to live for. The white men will trick us out of everything.'

'No.' Crazy About Horses indicated his people to put their weapons up, to return to the village. 'We must talk.'

Black Pete followed them on horseback, his rifle still pointed at Red Ant's head. Any second an arrow could get him in the back, but he hoped he would have time to pull the trigger before he fell. He wasn't sure what all that talk had been about.

At the entrance to his lodge the old chieftain beckoned Pete to step down and enter. The cowboy did so, taking Red Ant in with him. Most of the older Indians crowded in behind them. They didn't want to miss anything.

The pipe was lit and passed around and Pete,

sat cross-legged beside Red Ant, summoned up what he had of the Comanche tongue and said, 'Crazy About Horses, you were a friend to me once. Red Ant here has led your warriors against me. You can see I have beaten him fair and square. Now you have to make peace. The soldiers are coming. There is nowhere you can hide. I will help you make a treaty with them. They will assign you land. You can live there. The soldiers will give you blankets and canvas for your tepees and rations of food, like they do the Navajos and Apaches who have made peace.'

It took quite a while to persuade them and throughout Red Ant said not a word, just sat haughtily gazing into space, tightly bound in his ropes. Pete's rifle was across his knees aimed his way.

'We are agreed, Black Pit. You are a worthy enemy. You have killed too many of my warriors. We cannot go on.'

'I didn't want to kill 'em, you know that. It was them or us. Red Ant here won't listen to reason. He run off my cattle; killed my men. What could I do? Will he make peace now?'

Crazy About Horses spoke for some time to Red Ant, who sat, impervious, his eyes fierce and far-seeing. He did not want to surrender. Finally, however, he grunted and nodded.

'We will come down to make the treaty,' the old chieftain intoned. 'Red Ant will wipe off his warpaint. He will come with us.'

'Good. I will come and tell you when the time is due. I want to trust your word. I want to be a friend to you. I will release all these prisoners I have taken.' It was strange to Pete to be sat talking to these solemn-faced survivors of another age after fighting them for so long. 'I believe this will be good for the white and the red man. We will live at peace.'

'I hope so.' Crazy About Horses looked sadly at him. 'Will you be taking my ponies?'

'No. They are yours. You can keep ten of the cattle, slaughter 'em for beef. Thet should keep you goin' for a while. No need to go robbin' me or the Murchisons.'

He put up his rifle, pulled his knife, loosened the noose around Red Ant's neck, cut the bonds on his wrists, put out his hand to shake. Red Ant ignored him. 'Waal, ' he sighed, 'I guess me and my friends will be moseying on. Sure hope this feller won't change his mind and come after us. I still don't trust him.'

'He will not attack you,' Crazy About Horses said. 'He has cost our tribe too many lives. He will sit under the sun without food and water for three days and hope to find a vision of peace.'

'Sure hope he finds it,' Pete said, offering his hand to Crazy About Horses, who grasped it. 'Tell me, what is the significance of thet circular badge Red Ant wears on his forehead, the funny head-dress?'

'That is his courage,' Crazy About Horses said. 'That is the shield that protects him, the magic that bears him aloft. The plumes carry him light as the wind.'

'Guess they got the wrong kinda wind this time,' Black Pete said, a twinkle in his eye. 'Tell your son he is a noble warrior. But us whites are a set of skunks and he ain't a match fer us.'

The Comanches chuckled at these words, and

even Red Ant smiled, ruefully. 'My magic has failed me,' he said, and ripped the red wheel from his forehead, the plumes from his hair, tossing them into the smouldering fire. His topknot tumbled down, his silk-black hair falling to his dark muscled shoulders. Suddenly he was no longer arrogant, his head bowed, humbled.

Black Pete slapped his shoulder and got to his feet. 'Don't take it so hard. There ain't no stoppin' the Tide of Time. Y'awl know that in your hearts.'

He ducked out of the tepee, swung into the saddle, and rode out through the Comanches back to his 'Comancheros'.

'Set them Injins free,' he said. 'We're ridin' on through.'

FOURTEEN

The land looked desperately thirsty. There had been no rain for months. Even the mesquite looked like it was dying. And the sun blazed down. Louisa said she would most likely faint if she ever saw rain again. But, she didn't when it came. The lightning sheared through the night, the thunder rumbled like godly drums, and down it came, sheets of water, and they all ran out into the yard to catch it in their hats and let it streak down their faces.

When it kept coming for days they sat inside and watched it plod down, turning the dust to mud. Louisa tried to explain to Jim about the geography of North America, cold air rushing down from the arctic and colliding with the hot airstreams of the south which causes extremes of weather. This time the freak storm had turned the trickle of the Rio Grande into a wall of water and they heard news of terrible floods with hundreds of people drowned.

She took the opportunity of keeping him indoors, and his nose in the big old encyclopaedia she was teaching him to read from. They had worked their way through the 'Ps' and had reached: *polygamy – consists of a man having*

*more than one wife at the same time. It was
common among the barbarous nations of anti-
quity....* The subjects weren't very suitable, but it
made a change to The Bible. She explained that
the Comanche still practised this un-
Christianlike way of life, but it was possibly
necessary to their survival, which made some
sense to the boy.

'You sure are giving him an all-round eddy-
cation,' Pete said, as he went out to the barn. He
knew Jim would prefer to be out spinning his
lariat, or riding the grey filly, or helping him
grease the axles of the wagon which he was fixing
to carry food and supplies for the round-up.

'We will have to send him away to school soon,'
Louisa insisted. 'He has got to have the chance to
be somebody.'

Jim pulled a face at that, but bent diligently to
his words. It would have seemed more sense to
him if he could have learned the Comanche
language so he could coverse with Crazy About
Horses, if they ever met, about his many horses
and wives.

Black Pete guessed his wife was right. Louisa
didn't want her only son growing up to be a
bandy-legged cowpoke: it sure was a hard way to
make a few dollars, but they sure would miss him
if he was sent away to school.

He stocked up the covered wagon with branding
irons, horseshoeing equipment, a shovel and axe,
grain for the work team, a spare wagon wheel,
slickers, pots, skillets, ropes, guns, bullets, a
lantern and kerosene, coffee beans and a grinder,
a sourdough keg, salt, dried apples, the dried pony
meat, and a sack of pinto beans. His wife would

sort out the other supplies they would need. They were a pretty good team.

It was good. The rain had stopped. The land was greening over. The longhorns would have time to put on a little weight. Soon it would be time for the long trail.

Jim was in a high state of excitement because for the first time he was going out on the round-up with his father. His mother had insisted that if he was going, she, too, would go along. Louisa wasn't like other mothers. She was an excellent rider, and could cut out a calf for branding with the best of them.

She looked very trim as she straddled her pony in her split buckskin riding skirt, shirt, bolero, and straight-brimmed Spanish hat. Her eyes were glowing as she smiled at the Concho woman, whom Nathan had brought back, and who was also riding along. They all headed out towards the mountains at a dog-trot beside the rumbling chuck wagon, with Timothy handling the team.

They covered fifteen miles the first day and Pete said they would camp there and send scouting parties out to scour the coulées and canyons for the wild longhorns.

Jim was up at the crack of dawn, sitting around the fire with the men watching the coffee boil and bubble, and ran off to catch his grey filly in the remuda of spare saddle horses. He didn't want to miss any of the fun.

They didn't hang about, going off at a fast lope along the valley, heading for the hills. There wasn't time to admire the views. It was a long day of dashing pellmell after the men, leaping horses down hillsides, over fallen trees and boulders, splashing through the freshly-running streams, chasing the half-wild longhorns, climbing into arroyos, yelling wildly to hunt out strays; and, gathering the beasts together – bellowing bulls, calves bleating for their mothers – galloping alongside of them all, yipee-yaying, hooting, and driving them thundering back along the valley.

Jim watched his father, admiring the way he controlled Nimrod, turning him, backing him, dodging this way and that, spurring after a bull that made a dash for liberty. He had the air of knowing more about cattle-herding than any man in the field, a natural cowboy. And his mother was holding her pace with these wild frontier riders.

'For a lady, she makes a purty good cowboy,' he heard Nathan say.

Jim had been told to just ride along, watch what was going on, but not to get involed with the melée. By the mid-afternoon they had got plenty of cattle in the herd. There were a lot of bulls fighting and causing a commotion and milling about. He had never seen such a big herd. He had been specially warned to keep away from the fighting bulls.

However, the boy was anxious to help and show his prowess with the grey. He had been putting her through her paces around the ranch, herding up the milking cows, and the ponies, and he reckoned he could ride as well as any Comanch'.

There were a good many bunch-quitters in the herd – 'They are like me', Nathan told him. 'They don't like being fenced in,' – and when Jim saw one make a break for freedom, and that his dad and the others were busy elsewhere, he sent the

filly spurting after her. She had high-tailed it into
a narrow brushy canyon and Jim let out a happy
holler.

Too late Pete shouted at him to take care. Jim
was on to the beast as she turned at bay at the end
of the box canyon, swinging her great horns,
lunging at the filly, who reared with fright. Jim
was cornered, and the maddened cow tore at the
ground with her horns and prepared to charge.
Jim didn't know what to do.

There was a crashing in the brush as Pete on
his big black came through, his lariat in his hand.
The cow made a pass at him as he appeared, her
horns grazing his leg, as he dropped the rope over
them. As they passed in the opposite directions in
a wink of an eye the rawhide rope was tight. The
cow got the worst of it. Her head was brought to
snap alongside her tail. She was raised off the
ground. When she landed she popped like the lash
of a bull whip.

The cow didn't get up for a while. Pete got down,
took the rope off her head, coiled it, and climbed
into the saddle again. When the cow came to she
had lost a lot of her fighting spirit. She had
decided it might be best to head back to the herd.
Pete gave her a flick with the rope and set her off.

'You'd best not say nuthin' about this to your
mother,' Pete said.

Jim nodded, meekly, and trotted back after the
cow. Pete paused to roll a cigarette. 'Whew!' he
whistled. The incident had given him a fright. If
anything had happened to Jim he did not know
what he would have done. Maybe it was best, like
Louisa said, that they should send him off to
school. This was too dangerous a life.

*   *   *

After that, Jim, on his little filly, contented himself with watching. He liked the way the men would wind their horses through the herd, and how a horse could watch and outdodge a critter until, when the edge of the herd was reached, the horse would sort of pounce on the beast and send her sailing towards the 'cut' (where cattle were being held).

The branding had begun near the chuck wagon, for many of the cattle and calves had to be marked, and ropes were whistling through the air. Some of the cattle were so big that when the rope snapped taut on two occasions a man on horseback lost the contest and went down. Jim realized how tough his father had to be to throw that angry cow. However, none of the riders were hurt, and soon there was a fog of dust and the smell of burning hair and hide as, one after the other, the cattle were dragged across to the fire.

Jim confined his display of roping skills to catching the smaller calves, who had plenty of dodging skills. The filly was getting the hang of it and soon began to anticipate their twists and turns. Jim left the calf alone if it skulked behind its mother. But he dragged quite a few to the fire, himself.

That night, as he squeezed in among the men around the campfire, he felt pretty proud to be there beside his father. And, when he got into his tarpaulined blankets, and looked up at the brilliant overhanging stars, he reckoned it had been the best day of his life.

FIFTEEN

Lawman Elijah Jones had returned from San Antonio with good news. A detachment of cavalry would be dispatched to protect this section of the border. The Governor was having negotiations with the Army and, if the Comanche could be persuaded to come in to Broken Bow, two senators would arrive to accept their surrender, sign a peace treaty and assign them reservation lands.

'These things need chawin' over, as you know,' Elijah said. 'But if you can git Red Ant to come down out of the hills I'll arrange to have them senators here.'

Pete nodded. 'You reckon they'll get a fair deal?'

'Sure, why not? The Governor said to me he didn't see why they shouldn't stay in the mountains on the land they got. Make a big reservation and git an honest Injin agent in.'

'The only honest Indian agent I ever knew was put in a lunatic asylum,' Pete said. 'He made a fuss about the Cherokee's sacks of rations arriving filled with rocks. The suppliers reckoned he must be mad to want to treat the Indians square and got him put away. And that's true.'

'Nev-uh!' Elijah exclaimed. 'You gotta watch them durn suppliers, thet's fer sure. They're

96

crafty as coyotes. Don't you worry, Pete. Ah'll see Red Ant gits a fair deal.'

And so Pete rode back up into Los Muertos. He travelled with his men in case Red Ant, or any of his relatives, had decided to make a stand. When he neared the village he was beckoned forward by the guards and went on in alone.

A silence of defeat hung over the camp. Even the dogs seemed to have ceased their barking, the children their playing. Red Ant and the younger warriors hung around in a group and eyed him, sullenly. Only Crazy About Horses seemed pleased to see him, and they squatted in his lodge with the elders and smoked.

'I have been at war with the white men most of my life,' he said. 'I have come to the conclusion they cannot be defeated. The more we kill, the more they come and kill us in return. Now you say the soldiers are coming. They have many guns, and horses and cannons. They will not only kill my warriors, but our women and children and ponies. I believe the time has come to parley with you Texans.'

'I think so,' Pete said. 'Important white chiefs from Washington will come and make a treaty; give you land on which to live.'

The old man sighed, wearily, and sucked on the pipe. 'You Texans have always broken your promises in the past.'

'The days of fightin' are over,' Pete said. 'We gotta live at peace.'

Thus it came to pass that a raggle-taggle of some 500 Comanche trailed into the Wild Rose ranch some weeks later with their wounded on travois, overloaded ponies, bundles of skins and

cooking pots, children, dogs, and elderly, headed
by the mounted warriors who had washed off their
war paint. Pete welcomed and fed them, and the
next morning led them on into Broken Bow.

As they crossed Murchison's land his men rode
out to surround them, to laugh and jeer, but they
had heard what was going on, and followed them
into the town.

Outside Broken Bow were rows of canvas tents,
and a column of soldiers lined up on their horses,
and as they got nearer Pete saw that they were all
black soldiers. When the Comanche saw this they
stopped in their tracks. Red Ant looked angrily at
his father whose face had become a frozen mask.

'What's wrong?' Pete asked.

'This is an insult,' Crazy About Horses said. 'To
send the black whitemen to receive our surrender.'

Pete knew, with a sinking feeling in his stomach,
that the Comanche despised the black soldiers
even more than they despised the whites. He was
not sure why, perhaps on account that not so long
ago they had been slaves.

'C'mon,' he said, forcing a grin. 'They ain't gonna
attack you. You cain't go back now.'

Crazy About Horses saw the truth of this. It was
too late to run. If they did the black whitemen
probably would attack. He could see a Hotchkiss
cannon on its caissons pointed threateningly their
way.

A lone rider was heading towards them, and, as
he approached they saw that he was white. His
yellow scarf was fluttering in the breeze, and his
gold buttons and epaulettes gleaming, his navy
blue hat pulled rakishly to one side as he jogged up
and reined in.

'Captain Carpenter,' he called, introducing himself. 'In charge of the all-negro Tenth US Cavalry.'

'Yeah,' Pete drawled, leaning over his saddle-horn. 'We can see that. And the Comanches don't like it.'

'Yes, I have heard that they are worse racists than you southerners,' Captain Carpenter said, airily. 'Let's keep them moving, shall we? The senators are waiting to pow-wow.'

The Comanche seemed placated by Carpenter's white skin and began to move again. Glancing around Pete could see the fear and anxiety on the faces of the women and elderly, and a look of stoic disdain and distrust on the faces of the warriors.

Outside the flap of the main tent a table had been placed where the two senators were seated. They were dressed in tall silk hats and frock coats and cravats; fat and pompous, and, on this flat prairie beside the ramshackle town they looked out of place and ridiculous.

Behind them were stood most of the township people, who did not number all that many. Lawman Elijah Jones beckoned to the rough-looking cowhands to take their horses behind the line of soldiers. Pete, with a start of shock, saw Old Man Murchison and his two sons sitting alongside the senators. Hal, with his broken nose, leered at him. Pete chose to ignore him.

'This here's Pete Bowen, former Deputy US Marshal,' Elijah said, introducing him to the senators. 'At considerable personal risk he has persuaded these Comanche to sue for peace and has brought them down from the mountains.'

Pete nodded at the senators, dismounted, but

did not offer them his gloved hand. He turned to the Comanche and beckoned to them to sit in the dust and explained to Crazy About Horses who the two men in stovepipe hats were.

One of the senators, a bushy-bearded one – he never caught his name – rose and addressed the crowd, saying, 'We owe a debt of gratitude to Mr Murchison and Mr Bowen who have finally subdued these savages. Thanks to them, you settlers on this part of the frontier will be able to sleep in your beds without fear henceforth.'

'It was Bowen who brought 'em in, not Murchison,' a man in the crowd shouted, but the senator ignored him.

Pieces of paper were produced. Crazy About Horses was brought forward, given a quill pen, and shown where to make his mark. The senators signed beside it with a flourish and shook hands, posing for an itinerant photographer under his black cover to record the occasion.

'Can I see that treaty?' Black Pete asked of Captain Carpenter. 'Where 'zactly are you settling 'em?'

'You wouldn't understand it,' the Captain replied, shaking powder on the ink.

Everybody was in a festive mood and the Captain hurried away to organize the coming forward of the braves to throw down their rifles, lances, skull-crackers and bows. Crazy About Horses made signs for them to do so.

Murchison sat chatting to the senators, his keen beady eyes roving over Pete Bowen. He, too, was dressed city-style, clean linen and tie, frock coat and stovepipe trousers, but his hat was a low-crowned plainsman's, and he carried a revolver on his hip. Unlike his sons', his body was skeletal, and the flesh of his face seemed to be whittled to the bone. Folk couldn't help remarking how his prominent beaky nose gave him the look of some old eagle.

Suddenly Pete realized that the soldiers, with their gleaming black faces, had closed in on the disarmed Comanche and, at gunpoint, were putting shackles on the wrists and ankles of the warriors. The Indians were protesting, a howl of anger going up, but they were surrounded and helpless.

'What are you doin'?' Pete shouted. 'Where you taking these people? I was told they could stay in their own mountains.'

'Keep your nose out of it, Bowen,' Hal snarled. 'We all know you're a fuggin' Injin-lover.'

'Where they goin', I said?' Pete repeated, grabbing one of the senators by his stock, hauling him towards him. He felt his arms being grabbed on each side, his revolvers pulled from him, and he was held by the soldiers. He tried to struggle but it was no use.

'You mangy saddle-tramp,' the senator said, straightening his stock, securing his top hat, which had jolted over his nose. 'How dare you attack me? I could have you put in irons.'

Pete looked wildly for help from the lawman, but he, guiltily, avoided his eyes. 'Where are you takin' 'em?' he shouted. 'Thet's all I wanna know.'

'Florida,' the senator said. 'They will be marched to Louisiana and put on trains from there. A piece of land awaits them. Are you satisfied?'

'No, I ain't,' Pete said, kicking out, trying to get

the senator in the gut, knocking the table over, scattering ink and papers and men. 'You miserable lyin' snakes....'

He was pulled off and punched hard in the kidneys where it hurt. Crazy About Horses was watching with horror. Pete met his regard, and when he had regained some breath, panted out in Comanche: 'I did not know. I would not have done this. They two-timed me.'

'Where is this Florida?' Crazy About Horses was saying, sadly, as they put the chains on him.

'A thousand miles away. A durn mosquito-infested swamp they've found you,' – but he did not know the Comanche words to say it.

'We have been tricked!' Red Ant screamed, and, tearing a rifle from a surprised trooper, he smashed him in the face with it.

Red Ant was as yet unshackled, and, tumbling another soldier out of his saddle, like a mountain puma he had leapt upon the mount, and, hanging low on its neck, he was racing away before anybody could stop him, shots whistling about his ears. Soon he had become a spiral of dust on the plain, heading back towards his mountains.

They slung Pete in the town jail for twelve hours to cool off. The senators waived any charges against him, and by the time he was released they were on the stagecoach heading back to civilization, hurrying away from these lawless parts. Black Pete and his men could hear the Murchison bunch making merry in the saloon. They were sick at heart as they rode back in the moonlight across the silver sage to the Wild Rose ranch.

SIXTEEN

Two months or more in the saddle, heat, dust, thirst, mosquitoes, little sleep, and the possibility of attack by savage Indians, or rustlers, this was the prospect that faced cowpunchers going on a big cattle drive. All for $100 pay-off at the other end. But, all of Pete's men were eager to participate. It was a challenge. Not many men cared to go a second or third time. But, once completed, they could be considered men among men. They could walk with pride.

His first worry was to get the two thousand head of longhorns across the Murchisons' land. He would have to push them hard when it was best to move them gently. The greening of the land had put more meat on their bones. He did not want to lose it. But, who knew what those rattlesnakes might try. Most people were sure Old Man Murchison was behind a group of vigilantes calling themselves The Stranglers, who rode by night, lynching nesters who had dared to intrude on to their land, burning their houses, running off their stock. Abraham Murchison had a virulent hatred of sheep-herders, which was understandable, but most of the land was not legally his in the first place. Only by the law of the six-shooter.

Sure enough, a posse of his boys turned up on the second day out. They had eased the herd out into a long line about a dozen abreast, and when he saw the horsemen approaching, Pete turned Nimrod to meet them. He signalled Matthew and Miguel to go with him.

Slim McKenzie reined in his horse, and grinned at them, pulling aside his gambler's coat to reveal the handle of his Colt ready for action. 'You got permission to cross our land?'

'You gonna stop me?'

Pete could see Clay among the men in the background, his wisp of fair moustache, smiling slyly.

'You gonna leave that purty li'l wife of yourn on her own while you away?' Clay shouted. 'Ain't you worried about her?'

'She can take care of herself. And our ranch,' Pete growled. 'And she's got protection. I've told Estevan, if he sees any of you dogs sneakin' around, to shoot first, ask questions later.'

'You hear that?' McKenzie whooped. 'We're dogs now. You sure that Estevan ain't a wolf in sheep's clothing? I'd never trust a greaser. And a woman can get mighty lonesome.'

At that all his men howled and whistled, lecherously. Pete eyed them darkly, and shrugged. 'If all you got to do is exercise your foul mouths, we ain't. We got work ahead of us.'

He tugged at Nimrod's reins, and they trotted back and took up their positions at the head of the slow-moving column. He marked McKenzie and his men walking their horses alongside for a while, obviously looking at the brands, and, tiring of their fun, ride off into the distance. Even they

would not have dared to try to stop a rancher from
taking his herd to market. If they had Old Man
Murchison would have been unable to hold his
head up in the San Antonio Cattlemen's Club, or
even enter it. But they would have to keep a tight
armed guard on the herd at night. Nobody would
be getting much sleep.

Pete wouldn't have put it past those varmints
sneaking up in the night and trying to rustle some
of his herd. The nights, however, passed
uneventfully. The moon was full and it was like
silvery daylight, which maybe kept them off. The
cattle were sitting down peacefully as the boys
slowly rode the bounds, the Mexicans crooning
gentle lullabies. It soothed the beasts.

The coarse words of Clay still rankled in Pete's
mind and he was far from soothed. He wondered if
he had been right to leave Estevan behind. The
only others there were the Mexican farmboys. The
handsome young Spaniard was very attentive to
Louisa. He would help her with her chores, and
chatter gaily. It was more like the friendship of a
brother and sister, two people of the same
country. Or so he believed. He reckoned he could
trust Louisa. Anyway, Estevan had wanted to
come with them. Pete had wanted Louisa to take
Jim to her father's while they were away, but she
had refused. 'Somebody has got to hold on to our
ranch,' she had cried. 'Anybody could walk in here
and take it if we all go.'

Red Ant was on the prowl with vengeance in his
heart, but he seemed to have gone to join a band of
Comanches making war further to the west, or so
Pete had heard. He didn't like it. But danger was
the risk in this life. It was something you

constantly lived with. And Estevan was a good
man, fast with his gun, possibly as fast, or faster,
than Pete. And he was his friend. He was the right
one to leave. Wasn't he?

Pete tried to push the thoughts out of his mind
as unworthy of Louisa. He was already missing
his wife, and he wondered, sometimes bitterly,
why he had ever brought her to these parts,
chosen the life of a cowman.

They travelled on across this land of distances,
leaving Louisa and Jim and Estevan and the Wild
Rose ranch far behind them. It took them a month
before they were out of Texas. And most of the
time he was too busy to think of what was behind,
constantly riding on up front to scout the land,
look for a spot to halt that night, find the next
waterhole. Fortunately, the terrible storms had
made water one less problem.

The black boy, Timothy, had proved a capable
cook under Louisa's tuition, and would rumble the
chuck wagon on ahead of the herd to the chosen
campsite, so the boys would catch the appetizing
drift of bacon and beans cooking as they slowed
the longhorns down at the end of the day.

Pete had decided to make for the well-worn
Chisholm Trail, rather than break new ground.
And on the fortieth day out they arrived at Red
River Station to be confronted by the sight of
thousands of longhorns milling. Forty other
herds, numbering some sixty thousand head had
arrived before them, and had been hanging about,
their drovers unwilling to attempt to cross the
swollen floodwaters of the river.

'Never seen so many cows in my life!' Nathan
cried.

'What you gonna do?' Miguel asked, as they surveyed the brown turbulent waters rushing past.

Black Pete rolled a cigarette, jammed it into his clenched lips. 'Sonuvabitch,' he muttered. 'Last time through the herd easily waded it. I never thought of this.'

Miguel pushed his wide sombrero back to hang on his shoulders, revealing his bald bronzed dome, from which long hair hung, frontier-style, to his shoulders. His face was honed and burned almost ebony, indicative of his hard and muscled body, which was covered by the coarse striped blanket of mauve and brown colours, held by a thick leather belt, into which his revolver was stuffed. Pete had come to regard him as one of his best men, a fearless rider, who 'knew cows'.

'What would *you* do?' he said.

Miguel chewed on his long moustaches, idly flicked the rawhide quirt hanging from his wrist, and said, 'I would go over. We may lose some cows, maybe some men.'

'Reckon so,' Pete said. 'Cain't see no point in hanging around here. They all so jammed up, mebbe we can git through on that west side.'

They rode back to the chuck wagon, where Nathan and Matthew were stuffing their faces, taking first turn at eating, while the Apaches and the Mexicans kept the restless herd from mingling with the other beasts.

'C'mon, you lazy cusses. This ain't no time fer a rest. We gonna git this herd across afore nightfall.'

'It's crazy, Mr Bowen,' Matthew protested. 'It cain't be done. Look at thet water.'

'We looked, Matt, and we reckon it can.'

And into the water the herd were pushed and sashayed, bellowing and moaning, but holding their horns and noses high and swimming into the deep, the little calves bobbing next to their mothers, fighting the current that threatened to sweep them away, like the broken trees and heavy brush that was being swirled along. It looked as if for hundreds of miles everything that grew had been plucked out by the roots to be swept hurtling along.

It was only the cowboys who couldn't swim, or most of them, and they clung with trepidation to their ponies, as they headed for the other bank, some being swept off and having to hang for dear life to their saddles, and let the pony haul them along. Half-way across, however, things were going wrong. The longhorns had bunched up into a milling circle, and were drifting downstream.

'Ye gods,' Pete said, envisaging the loss of his herd, kneeing Nimrod towards them through the foam. He had no clear idea of what to do, but acted by instinct, clambering out of the saddle on to the backs of the jammed longhorns. It was like walking a huge moving and slippery raft of logs. Managing to balance, he made his way across them, jumped on to the only big steer he could see on the yon side, and, kicking his spurs into him, like he would a horse, pulling on his horns, rode him to the far bank. He looked back to see that the herd had straightened out and was following him ashore.

Water slushing in his boots, he jumped down and gave a whoop of triumph, and beckoned Nathan to bring the remuda of fifty spare cow ponies across. They were strong swimmers and actually seemed to enjoy the crossing, and Nathan grinned at him as he arrived.

The problem now was to get the wagon over safely. They would hardly be able to continue if they had no supplies. They could see the white of Timothy's eyes: they rolled with extreme agitation as he urged the team into the water, Miguel leading at their head. Again it looked as if they would be swept away, but they battled on, and Pete recovered Nimrod and swam him out to meet them with ropes attached to the ponies. Somehow or other they struggled the wagon over to the bank where Indian Territory began.

It was with somewhat contemptuous whoops and waves that the merry band hollered back to the men and their herds watching them on the far Texas side.

It was an exhausted gang of men who dried out their clothes and supplies around the campfire that night. Pete aired out his blankets as best he could and rolled up in them to try to get a few hours' sleep before going on the 'graveyard watch'.

They had made it halfway, but there was still 300 or so miles of wild lawless territory to cross. A month or more of travelling before they got to Dodge.

SEVENTEEN

Black Pete had known the land of the Indian Nations as a vast tract of mountains, lakes and grasslands into which few whites ventured. He had helped form the Cherokee Light Horse and fought with them against the North in the War. He had been trail-boss on early cattle drives across it. And two years before he had wandered its Black Mesa mountains and its southern length through winter snows on the trail of the evil Comanche 'breed, Blue Jay Rogan.

The five civilized tribes, the Cherokees, Chickasaws, Choctaws, Creeks and Seminoles, had been given lands here 'in perpetuity', with their own constitutions, courts and schools, but things were changing fast. Modern life was pressing hard upon them. Settlers were pressing to move in on their land. The first railroad, the MKT, or Katy, was thrusting southward across the Nations, and that year, 1873, reached the Red River near Colberts Ferry.

This area, west of the Mississippi, was rich in mineral wealth, as yet unexploited, but that year the Choctaws had agreed to Italians carrying out deep-shaft mining for coal. Oil had been discovered on Chickasaw lands. Soon drilling would begin. One day the Osages would become the richest tribe in the United States. The tribes were sitting in the path of progress.

Pete was as much a part of that tide of progress as any man. He was ambitious to be a successful cattleman. He was intent on selling his cows, getting money in the bank. But, he had seen the way Indians were being swindled and he didn't like it.

He had also been surprised by that vast conglomeration of herds at Red River Station, that maelstrom of horn and leather. He had not realized how competitive the cattle business had become. Every rancher in Texas, it seemed, was sending his cattle north. At least they had got a head start on those galoots. Later he heard that the herds on that south bank had all stampeded and intermingled and it had taken the trail crews ten days to cut them back into their original herds.

Stampede! It was the one thing the trail bosses feared. Pete awoke one night to the ground reverberating his eardums. A pounding of hooves. He was up in an instant, pulling on his boots, hollering: 'All hands and the cook!' He had no need to yell. They knew what to do. They were running for their horses stumbling in the dark the same as him, as a flash of lightning scorched the earth and fizzled around their ears. It was this that had set the herd off. There had been a tension in the air all night.

They might look an ungainly bunch, but those longhorns could run. A state of communal panic gripped them, two thousand sets of horns clashing and hooves pounding as they rumbled along towards the camp. Pete, Nathan and Miguel, on the first ponies they could get hold of, were making a blind dash towards the point. The two Apaches and Mexican, who had been on herd duty, were already galloping along the sides. Pete cut across and reached the head of the herd, slashing his slicker at the crazed leading animal's head, trying to turn him.

He glimpsed Miguel cracking his bullwhip, and, on his other side, young Nathan, shouting and hallooing in the turmoil of thunder and rain. It was no good. They wouldn't turn. After a deal of galloping, Black Pete pulled his .44, aimed at the leading stampeder's head, crashed a bullet into his brain, bringing him down. Two more steers tripped and went down with him. The herd surged over them. It had worked. With the leader gone they were turning.

Nathan was slapping his coiled lariat to turn the leader, when Pete saw him fall: carried away on a tossing of horns. Another streak of forked lightning illuminated the darkness as they galloped madly along. He saw Miguel ride into the deathly surge of wild-eyed steers, pluck Nathan from the back of one of the creatures, spur to the front and clear.

Gradually they eased the animals into a slow milling circle and tried to settle them down, hold them still against the cannon rumble of thunder. Any moment they could go again. In the morning they counted their losses. Twenty critters dead. A mess of broken horns and bones. At least they would be eating fresh beef for a day or two before it putrefied in the heat.

It was a bad omen. Black Pete sat Nimrod and eyed the leading steers, viciously. It looked like a little squad of them was just waiting to set the others off. Like they were saying to each other 'Let's git ready to break'. Should he shoot them now? Or was he going crazy?

Nathan was unhurt, in fact, elated by his experience. He claimed his bentwood stirrup had broken causing him to fall. Pete was more worried about his cows. Once a herd had stampeded anything could set them off, a prairie grouse flapping up, even a cowboy lighting a cigarette.

The stampede had gone for three miles. Each beef could have lost up to fifty pounds in the hot night. If it happened again they would arrive at the railhead looking a real stringy bunch.

On they went across rolling yellow grassland, day after day passing, the only breaks in the tedium of sitting in a hard saddle for sixteen hours a day being sightings of wolves, or elk, wild horses and, occasionally, the last of the herds of buffalo that had once turned the plains brown. Frequently Indians, in groups, or singly, would ride up to them and Pete, and Miguel, would ride out to parley. The Indians had become used to the cattle drovers and could usually be appeased with the gift of a beef, which they would slaughter on the spot. On one occasion they met a troop of the fierce Kiowa, and Pete asked them in their own language if they had any news of his friend, Trailing the Enemy. They looked uneasy and said they believed he had been wiped out by the Long Knives, and, with coyote yelps, galloped off.

At night they could get little sleep, They had to ride herd soothing the cattle. Exhaustion was beginning to take its toll on the grimy long-haired men. They had been driving for nearly two months when the cattle scented water. It was a hell of a job to slow them down so they didn't stampede right across the Cimarron River. It was the end of Indian Territory. On the other side lay Kansas.

'What 'n hell are them buffalos skulls?' Matthew asked when they had forded to the north side.

'That marks the trail that cuts off to the west up to Dodge.'

'Wouldn't it be easier to go north to Abilene?'

'Nope,' Pete said. 'Too much trouble with the Kansan settlers. This way it ain't goin' t'be easy either. No water for a hundred miles 'til we reach the Arkansas.'

'A hundred miles. It ain't possible. The critters will go blind and crazy from thirst,' Matthew protested. 'I say it's best to go to Abilene.'

'And I'm givin' the orders. We follow that line of skulls to Dodge. We'll push 'em hard, push on 'til after sundown. Tomorrow we'll rest 'em in the noonday heat. We gotta make double time. We gotta do that hundred miles in four days. Let's go. What are we waitin' for?'

Black Pete and his 'Comancheros' did it. They lived on black coffee and chewed 'baccy and even rubbed it in their eyes to keep them awake. A few puddles of rainwater helped the cattle along. And there, finally, was the River Arkansas. And, as the cattle watered, Nathan came whooping back on his pony because he had seen not far off across the plain the clapboard houses of Dodge City, and the black clouds of smoke from a locomotive on the cross-continental railroad. They were there.

The triumph was short-lived for Pete. What they called the big Depression of '73 had hit the land. There had been a glut of some 250,000 cattle pushed north the previous year. The banks had closed. Money was not being paid out. After much finagling, he was lucky to find a buyer for the herd. By the time he'd cleared his debts, paid off his cowboys, he would have made a grand profit on the year of 500 dollars. It was a bitter pill. He had practically given the herd away.

EIGHTEEN

'It sure makes you understand why some fellas turn to robbin' banks,' Black Pete said, hanging over the bar, looking out through the batwing doors into the harsh sunlight, and across the wide grassy street at a cabin with the legend BANK over its barred and bolted doors. 'Them bastards over there.'

The boys huddled around him, moodily. Was he suggesting that they turn bad? They could hardly blame him. All that work, all that planning, all that fighting off the Comanche, how was he going to buy enough supplies to look after his family for the winter while he cut out another herd of wild longhorns? They had all hoped to be going back with him. They had come to see themselves as a unit, had imagined he would look after them, give them employment, if not riches, for a while.

'Waal, ain't no use whining. Guess I ain't the only one. Look at them poor farmers out there. They cain't git any credit. Cain't even git the money of their own outa the bank. The whole durn nation seems to have gone broke. At least I got what little cash I got for the herd in gold. A letter of credit wouldn' have been much use.'

He had been so busy the past days trying to get

a price for the beeves he hadn't even had time to take a bath, haircut or shave. He was dusty and unkempt, his leather leggings in tatters, his boots busting at the seams.

He guessed he didn' oughter: he hadn't had a whiskey in two years. But, hell. Today he needed one. He poured himself a shot from the bottle and tipped it to his mouth. The fiery liquid seemed to ease through his veins, bringing a glow. It had been a long time. 'Yeeee-hooooo!' he yelled, slapping a golden eagle down. 'Fill 'em up again.'

He slapped Timothy on the back. 'You made a durn fine cook, you sure did, Tim. And a good enough cowboy, too. I'm sorry for you fellas. I was hoping we could all head home. It looks like this is the end of the trail.'

'Aw, thet's all right, Mistuh Bowen. We can all pick up a cowpunchin' job some place. We ain't got no family to support like you.'

'You were a good foreman, Matt. And you, Miguel, the best, the whole durn lot of you. Guess I'm gonna have to sell your chuck wagon, Tim, and the remuda, Nat, and see if I cain't raise any more cash legal-like 'fore I head back to Texas. Sure is a hard life, ain't it? Yassir.'

They looked a trifle uneasy. They had never seen him drink before. They had heard he had been pretty wild when he was younger. Never sure what he might do. He had been served a raw deal. But, he was one of many. He was tough enough to pull through, to get started again.

'Hope you boys ain't figurin' on causin' any mayhem,' a loud voice said. 'I'd be obliged if you would take them shootin' irons off and leave 'em behind the bar in accordance with the city ordinances.'

Pete turned to see a stout middle-aged man, cleanly dressed, clean shaven, his moustache neatly clipped, a star indicating his office as city sheriff pinned to his shirt chest. 'Howdy,' he said, offering his hand. 'My boys won't cause no trouble. We ain't thet sort.'

'Us Texans never give up our guns,' Nathan yelled. 'Not 'til we're in our coffin.'

The sheriff's eye twitched as he regarded them. He looked a nervous man. 'I should warn you boys –'

'Sure,' Pete drawled. 'If thet's the city ordinances. Put your guns up, boys, like the man says. He's got his lousy job to do.'

'Thanks,' the sheriff nodded, as Pete began to unbuckle his gunbelt.

'Thet's OK,' Pete said, his teeth clenching on a cheap cigar as he paused. A shabby-looking man had pushed through the swing doors and he had a shotgun in his hands and it was aimed at the sheriff's back.

Pete hefted the sheriff aside, but the man swung the shotgun and blasted him. KER-POW!

Pete's .44 crashed out simultaneously and the man hit the deck, a bullet in his heart. He grunted like a pig, and died.

The sheriff was in a bad way, too. He was lying on the rough floorboards, peppered with shot. Pete knelt beside him. He might pull through.

'Who was he?' Pete asked.

'Durn settler. I strung up his brother t'other day. He shot a man in a card game. Guess he was after revenge.'

'I cain't abide a back-shooter. Worse than a

rattler sneakin' up on ya. Go for a doctor, Nathan. Gotta get the lead outa this man. How long you bin in office, Sheriff?'

'Three months. It's about as long as any man lasts,' the sheriff said, as Pete examined him. 'I'm finished now. It's my right arm. He's done it in.'

Pete carefully tore away the sleeve. The arm was a bloody mess. 'Yeah,' he whistled. 'You won't be doin' a lot of gun-feudin' from now on. How much do they pay for sheriff?'

'Hundred dollars a week. Nobody will take it for less. You want the job, you're welcome.'

'I cleaned up Abilene once. Mebbe I can do the same fer Dodge.' Pete grinned, the whiskey spinning his brain. 'Sure is better than seven dollars a week as a cowpoke. Give me that badge, Sheriff. I'll telegraph Judge Parker to swear me in.'

NINETEEN

'Oh, my God!' Louisa gave a little gasp of dismay as she read the telegraph.

'What's wrong, Ma?' Jim asked, anxiously.

Louisa read the words out to him: *Bad price for herd. Must stay Dodge as lawman to raise cash. Love to both. Pete.*

'Lawman?' Jim echoed.

'Yeh' – she heard a snigger and felt a man standing looking over her shoulder at the message – 'he'll be whoopin' it up with those li'l hoorhouse gals.'

Louise looked around into the pale, stunted features of Clay, the trickle of gingery moustache above a loosely grinning mouth. She didn't want her boy to hear such words and snapped, 'Go down to the corral, Jim, and watch the horses. I'll be along soon. I've some more shopping to do.'

As Jim ran off, she started away from Clay along the wooden sidewalk that edged the dusty main street of Broken Bow. Clay, however, clomped along beside her. 'Ain't you heerd about what went on when he was lawman of Abilene? He kept some li'l under-age brothel gal in his jail for his private usage. Molly they called her. He rode off into the nations with her, sold her to an

120

Injin to save his skin.'

'You're a liar!' Louisa spun on him. 'My husband would never do such a thing. He has never done a cowardly dishonourable thing in his life.'

'Heh? You bin lookin' at him thru rose-tinted glasses. Thet fat Maria down the bordello could tell you about the special treatment she give him in Mexico.'

Louisa flushed, angrily. But more than anger was the deep sense of dismay in her. A huge emptiness and loss filled her soul. She felt abandoned. She looked at the snarl of spite on the face of her persecutor, saw people in doorways listening to the scene. She did not want to hear any more. As if lost in a maze she spun away and hurried down a side alley-way.

Clay pursued her. He was enjoying this. He caught up with her as she turned into another alley-way at the back of the stores and they were alone. He grabbed her arm and slammed her up against a wall, pressing on to her. 'What makes you so damn precious? If Pete's enjoyin' hisself, why don' you, eh?'

Louisa struggled to escape, turning her head away from the foul-smelling mouth. But the evil words continued to drill into her.

'Hear tell thet Li'l Moll's back in Kansas ridin' with them Doolin bank robbers. Mebbe Pete's figurin' to meet up with her agin?'

'Get off me!' Louisa screamed, as the fingers of one of Clay's hands dug into her breast, and the other clawed to tear away her dress. But Clay's lust had given him strength and he had her tight.

'C'mon you gorgeous Mex bitch. You ain't had it for two months and you ain't goin' to be gittin' it fer another six. You need it, same as any bitch does. This time you goin' git it from me.'

Clay had torn her blouse apart and was slavering over her. Louisa was fighting him, desperately, her eyes flashing, her black curls tumbled down across her cheek. She heard a cool voice say, 'It's you who's going to be getting it, *señor*,' and knew a sweet sense of relief.

Estevan had been playing cards in the saloon when Jim had come racing in, hissing, 'There's something the matter with Ma. It's that Clay.'

Estevan had jumped to his feet and gone running. Now the handsome young Mexican stood there watching the scene, his blue eyes vividly intense beneath his mop of curls. He could not resist a tremor of desire in himself as he saw Louisa's pale exposed breasts, her bare thigh, as the cowhand clawed at her. He was almost tempted to let the scene run on a little longer. Wasn't this what he himself had wanted for so long to do?

He smiled as he saw the surprise on Clay's ugly mug. 'You enjoy yourself, *señor*? Hope I not disturbing you. Perhaps you would like to step away from the lady, you shit-eating cur. I don' think she likes your filthy hands to touch her.'

Clay stepped away from Louisa, perplexed. The Mexican was standing there, mocking him, a revolver holstered across his chest. He had heard he was fast. He licked his lips with fear as he hesitated. But the frustration and anger in him made him go for his .45 on his belt.

Ka-room! The alleyway echoed to one shot. Clay was knocked backwards, a slug in his chest, to lie in a heap of boxes.

Louisa could not help herself. She ran to Estevan and buried her face in his chest. Nor could Estevan help himself. He circled his arm around her tightly, and bent to gently kiss her hair. 'It's over,' he whispered. 'You're all right.'

Over her shoulder he kept an eye on Clay, who was trying to raise himself, blood seeping from his shirt. He was tempted to finish him off. The sneer had come back on to the cowhand's face as he watched them.

'I see!' he gasped out, and almost laughed. 'It's you she's gittin' it from.'

Estevan went up to him and kicked him in the face with his spurred boot. 'What does it take to shut your filthy mouth?' he shouted.

The sheriff, Elijah Jones, and some townsmen, had crowded into the alley-way as Clay collapsed. 'This man tried to rape her,' Estevan said. He holstered his revolver, took his snakeskin jacket off and draped it around Louisa's shoulders to cover her. He put an arm around her and pushed through the throng back towards Jim.

The boy ran and hugged her waist. 'Ma, are you all right?'

'Sure I am,' she said, forcing a smile. 'We better be going home.'

It sounded strange saying that – the 'we' and the 'home' – not with Pete but with Estevan.

TWENTY

Red Ant had climbed high into the south-western stronghold of the Mountains of Death. He had spent many days meditating and praying alone in the vastness trying to summon up once again his warrior spirit. As he sang and chanted, his arms wide, he vowed never to abandon it again to the whites. He also needed a red bead shield for his headband, and this took time to make, and plumes for his head-dress. The Texas bird of paradise was difficult to catch, but with patience and cunning he succeeded in hitting several with his slingshot as they bickered and engaged in aerial battles. Their long tail streamers made a magnificent top plume that would bear him and his horse aloft. Then he went in search of recruits.

His band numbered only a dozen Comanches, but, anger in their hearts at what he had told them, they set off on a trail of carnage, riding through the parched land, hitting scattered settlements, giving no quarter, burning, raping, slaughtering, and riding on. They travelled with such speed that in seven days they had covered 400 miles. Due to the treachery of the white politicians some thirty-five settlers were cruelly murdered in Red Ant's revenge.

Eventually they reached the western plains where the greatest of the Comanche chiefs, Quanah Parker, the blue-eyed and dark-skinned half-breed, was mustering a war party of 700 strong. With them he would war against buffalo hunters and the US soldiers until the Comanche was lord of the plains again ... or so he believed.

TWENTY-ONE

Four months had passed since Pete had ridden off
with the herd. Maybe three or four months more
would pass before she saw him again. Louisa
twisted and turned under the sheet on their
marital bed in the hot night, the bed that had seen
so much love. The thoughts kept taunting her and
she tried to push them away. What if it were true
about the fair-haired American girl, Molly? What
if Pete was with her at this very moment? He had
spoken to her before about the girl, about how she
married a Kiowa, Trailing the Enemy, and how
the three of them tracked down Blue Jay. But,
what had he been doing with her in Indian
Territory in the first place? It had never occurred
to her to ask him that. She had trusted him
implicitly, as she expected him to trust her. He
was the only man she had ever loved, ever
wanted, and she had believed he felt the same
way about her. But Clay's words seemed to come
whispering to her through the night, about Molly,
about Maria. And it was true what he had said:
she was a woman, she did need a man's arms
about her: she longed for it. She tried to think of
Pete, but an image of Estevan crept into her mind,
and she twisted in the sheet again.

When they had returned to the ranch that day he had been very attentive to her, and, when they were alone, he had tried to kiss her. She had refused him, told him they could only be like sister and brother, that she believed in her marriage vows. Since then, he had kept his distance. He came from a good family and was extremely courteous. But, sometimes, as they sat alone she could feel those vivid eyes of his burning into her.

Her son, Jim, idolized Estevan, almost as much as he did his father. Estevan was dashing and gay, a true *cabalero*. He was always laughing and playing games with the boy, whereas Pete could be moody and serious. Estevan had a huge appetite for life. Pete had seen too much death in his time: it had hardened him. Estevan had killed men, too, and there was something in his past in Mexico he would not speak about. But, he cast it off as of no consequence. He was good to the boy, took him out on the range, helped him with his lessons, joking with him as if he was a kid brother. He had not tried to kiss her again.

What was she thinking about Estevan for? Why couldn't she sleep? She leaned on one elbow, lit the lantern, reached for Pete's letter to read it a hundredth time.

My darling Louisa, it began ... *them sonuvabitch bankers ... looks like this is going to be a tough town to tame ... Judge Parker wants me to do the full six months term ... going after bounty ... should have $2,000 saved by the time I return ... please take the boy back to your father's ranch and put him to school ... I am worried about you both ... I feel like I am a man*

*torn apart when I am away from you ... you are
the dearest person in the world to me ...
Your loving husband....*

Louisa's tears dripped on to the letter making the
ink run. She turned out the lantern, buried her
face in the pillow. 'Oh, Pete,' she cried. 'You
should not leave me.'

TWENTY-TWO

Wild Rose ranch was so called because of a creek from which their life-giving stream of water flowed and in which wild roses grew, perhaps still do. Where the water flowed from the mountainside as a spring, a short distance from the ranch house, there was a natural cave, which Louisa had walled over. In there Louisa kept perishables and made cheeses from their goats' milk. It was cool and shady and a wonderful refuge from the heat of the sun. It was blazing down outside, more than 100°F. The Mexican workers were taking their siesta, Jim was doing his studies in the house, Estevan was working in the barn, and the Concho woman was doing the washing along the stream. It was very quiet. Louisa was determined not to quit the ranch. Sure Red Ant might be bent on revenge, or even the Murchisons wanting to cause trouble over Clay's death. There always had been trouble and there always would be. A stubborn streak in Louisa said they would not drive her away.

She heard footsteps scrambling up the path and reached for her rifle. But it was Estevan, his matt of curls, his cheerful smile. 'Hey,' he said. 'It's cool in here. It's too hot to work.'

He watched her as she worked at the damp cheeses, her full body in the loose blouse and skirt. Louisa could feel his eyes upon her. 'Don't,' she warned herself; warned him.

The attraction between them seemed to fill the air like static electricity, crackling; her heart pumping, her thoughts spinning, and, as if unable to resist, she turned her dark eloquent eyes to him interlocking with his violet ones. It was no good. She was in his arms; she was kissing him; and gradually, slowly, they slipped down to lie on the hard rock floor together.

It was the first of many such afternoons of lovemaking for Louisa and Estevan. It was as if they were desperate to suck love's nectar dry before that moment which, as the months passed, drew ever nearer – the return of her husband.

'You must go before he gets back,' she said. 'He will kill you.'

'You must come with me. We will go back to Mexico,' Estevan said. 'I do not want to kill him.'

'No, I cannot,' Louisa said, and kissed his handsome, delicate features. 'He is Jim's father. You must go.'

'I cannot,' Estevan said, glumly. 'I want you so. As they say in our country, what good is paradise to a man if he has no Eve?'

TWENTY-THREE

It sure was one wild town this Dodge City. The long, low, plank buildings, mud-chinked log cabins, and tents, had proliferated shambolically since Black Pete had stopped off there two years before when Blue Jay and his boys had murdered four soldiers. It was in line to becoming one of the busiest trailhead towns. There were already ten saloons, a lush casino and a seasonal population of 2,000 or so. The railroad was shipping out settlers, roughnecks, and all kinds of shady characters from the east. And shipping back wagons filled with livestock. In spite of the financial recession the herds that had been left behind at the Red River kept on coming and were sold off at rock-bottom prices, or were trailed on up to Wyoming. The town was full of wild and angry cowboys, professional gamblers, carpet-baggers, and, inevitable as vultures around a carcase, a flock of even wilder women intent on stripping the cowboys of their cash. One known as Galloping Jane had walked down Main Street naked for a bet, cool as a cucumber and it had been Pete's job to arrest her and lock her up for the night. And on every train other girls, some as young as thirteen, arrived to sell their bodies.

Pete had to round up the under-age ones and send them packing.

As usual the Bible-punchers among the population tut-tutted at the pony racing, gun-shooting and wild fornicating antics, but their stores reaped a nice profit from the summer and fall invasion of the Texans who swaggered around their streets.

As a Texan, himself, Pete could generally get on well with the trail crews. If anybody got feisty he tried to settle it with a fist crack to the jaw. But, on three occasions he had been forced to draw his .44s. And when he drew his instinct was to kill. And what with the knifings and muggings Boot Hill cemetery was getting full.

'The richest man in this town's thet durn undertaker,' he muttered to Nathan and Miguel, whom he had appointed his deputies, as they watched the hearse, its horses' black ostrich plumes dancing, being driven slowly out of town again.

The closure of the banks had eased off and credit was beginning to circulate again. He had just received yet another message from Judge Parker ordering him to leave the policing of Dodge to his deputies, and to get after the Doolin gang. As a Deputy Marshal he guessed he had no alternative but to obey. The Doolins had given up robbing banks as a hayseed activity. There was raw gold coming out of Colorado being shipped east. They had turned to train-robbing as a more profitable operation.

Pete looked at the telegraph with distaste. It wasn't just that the Doolins were a pretty tough bunch of one-time Irish hill-billies, it was that

Molly was riding with them. And she wasn't just holding the horses. She was going in there and killing. There was a $1,000 bounty on her head alone.

Pete shook his head sadly. That gal had had a lot of potential. She must have taken Trailing the Enemy's death real bad. For a short while she had been Pete's lover and friend. He didn't look forward to bringing her back to hang.

'I got orders to ride out,' he told them. 'You boys don't drink too much whiskey while I'm gone. And watch your backs. There's some mean cusses around.'

TWENTY-FOUR

The heads of bison and bighorn sheep, trophies of antelope and Indians, and the biggest set of longhorns ever seen in the territory, from a famous lead-steer, Ole Faithful, who had been spared on several occasions to be brought back and set the pace on yet another cattle drive to the railheads, before he, too, was cut into steaks, looked gloomily down from the walls of the Murchison mansion. On one wall was a panoramic oil-painted view of a herd on the move across the prairies beneath louring skies by Charles Ives, one of the most expensive modern artists (they had paid him all of $26 for it). There was little doubt about how this family had come by its wealth.

Abraham Murchison sat in his big carved oak and horn chair at the head of a long highly-polished refectory table. He too, with his gaunt cheeks, prominent beak, and shock of grey hair, looked like some trophy of other times. He sat, erect, in his high white collar and black frock coat. His beady eyes bored like gimlets into his sons who sat sprawled in their dusty range clothes.

'This panic ain't gonna last forever,' he lectured them. 'We won't send the herd north this summer.

We'll hold 'em back. We ain't gonna go broke. Why you think I spend most my time in San Antone? That's where the information is. We got enough in the bank to wait for better times. What you boys gotta concentrate on is keeping back these upstart settlers who think they can move on to my land.'

Hal's whiskey-inflamed face broke into a grin. 'Sure, Paw, ain't we awready run 'em out? Once The Stranglers ride nobody hangs about.'

'Or, mebbe they do hang,' his younger brother, George, tittered. 'Geddit?' Hal gave a weak smile and frowned at him.

The old man gave a contemptuous, 'Hrmph! What about Pete Bowen? What about the Wild Rose ranch? If you boys had had any guts you would have moved in there afore of him, Comanch' or no Comanch'.'

'Don' reckern he'll be comin' back, Paw,' George whined. 'Heard tell he bin wiped out in the slump.'

'He'll be back,' Hal said. 'He got hisself a US Marshal's job up in Kansas. It won't last forever. He'll be back. He got a wife and kid here, ain't he?'

'Yeah,' – again George giggled – 'you heerd what goin' on over there with thet Estevan Ochoa, whatever he called?'

'All the more reason for him to be back.'

'Serve him right for marryin' a greaser,' Murchison spat out, a look of disgust on his face. 'I fought the Mexicans, pushed them back to their proper borders. And now Texans start marryin' em. Before long we'll be a mongrel race. You boys ever marry a Mexican or a nigger I cut you off without a penny, you hear? We gotta keep our race pure.'

'What about your cattle baron fren, Mistuh

Granville Stuart? He married a true blue Shoshone gal, didn' he? Got hisself seven mixed-blood brats at the last count,' George said. 'Nobody say nuthin' 'bout him.'

'Thet's 'cause he's got the same idea as Paw,' Hal laughed. 'Pizen sheep. Run homesteaders off the range.'

Abraham scowled at George, his brows veritably bristling. 'You thinkin' bringin' an Injin squaw this house, son? That would be the last thing you ever did. The pair o' you disgraced my name enough. And listen here, I done put an advertisement in one them eastern newspapers for two nice college gals of good family. I'm gonna bring 'em out here and marry 'em to you two. It's time I had some grandchildren. This family's got a proud name that's gotta go on. We gonna git some refinement. I had enough of you two sittin' around on your asses in the saloon all day throwing my money away on whiskey and poker and whores.'

'Aw, Paw,' George said, hanging his head, unable to meet the stern old patriarch's eye. 'Who bin tellin' you these tales?'

'We don' wan' no damn college gals,' Hal thundered. 'That's fer sure. We happy as we are.'

'You do as I tell you,' the old man cried. 'Don't think I couldn't take my belt off an' give the pair of you a good whuppin'.'

'We men grown, Paw. You cain't talk to us like this.'

'Men! The two of you couldn't knock Bowen down when you had the opportunity. He's a better man than the both of you.'

'It was a lucky punch,' Hal moaned, feeling his jaw.

At this point Slim McKenzie eased himself into the room. He had obviously been listening at the half-open door for there was a sly grin on his long features. 'What about the one that broke your nose?' he laughed.

'You ain't got no need to talk,' Abraham said, sternly. 'You should have stepped in there. You're supposed to be the fast-shooter? Ain't that what I pay you for? Or are you as yaller as these two?'

McKenzie settled his lean body into a chair, pulled his long-barrelled Colt Frontier from his belt, spun the cylinder, and for seconds the weapon's barrel and the slits of his green eyes were aimed at the old man, glinting in the dying sunlight. 'I ain't yaller,' he said. 'I'm biding my time. He's fast. And that Estevan's faster. You all know that.'

Abraham Murchison sat transfixed, until Slim crashed the gun down on the polished table, leaned back on two legs of the chair, and crossed one handtooled black leather boot over his knee, mockingly rocking there. Few men had called him yellow and lived.

'The point is you're being paid good money to lead my men and look after these boys,' Murchison said. 'I agree we gotta go careful with Bowen. Word's got to me that he's pally with Judge Parker, the Hangin' Judge. He got some kinda influence with the Governor, too, for what he did bringing them Comanche in, and destroyin' the Comancheros. Folk got reason to be grateful to him. But, to me, he's just a thorn in the side. He gotta go.'

'I'll get him,' Slim drawled, loosely swinging a golden dollar fixed to a chain on his flashy silver vest. 'When he shows up again in these parts.'

'Yeah, make sure you do. And you boys, always remember to wear masks when you ride with The Stranglers. We don't want folk to know who's behind that vigilante mob.'

'Don't worry about us,' Hal growled. 'Bowen'll have to pass through Broken Bow and across our land on his way back. We'll git him. Nobody breaks my nose and gits away with it.'

'Yeah,' George said, flicking dust off his piebald waistcoat, trying to look tough. 'An' with him gone we'll soon run that greaser Estevan back to his side of the border. And send the whore and her kid back to where they belong.'

'Make sure you do. I didn't fight for this land to see it taken from me,' Murchison said, as a serving maid brought in a platter of beef. 'Now about those college gals....'

Hal and his brother groaned. 'Aw, Pa.'

TWENTY-FIVE

Christmas had come and gone. The Doolins had been brought to justice. But things had gone bad. Nimrod had gotten killed. And it had not been easy with Molly. He did not want to think about that. He wanted to put it all behind him as he drifted south through the Washita valley and across the great plains. It was good to leave the blizzards of snow behind him. The air tasted cool, but the sky was clear blue and the sun shining as, after weeks in the saddle, he reached the south-west. He had bought a rough work horse in the last small town he rode through. And, if his eyes weren't deceiving him, weren't those the Mountains of Death, gaunt and dark, looming up? Wasn't that cluster of houses on the plain the town of Broken Bow?

Folk watched him, curiously, as his tired horse plodded in, two settlers' wives in sun-bonnets speaking animatedly, looking at him, and hurriedly moving away as he dismounted. Wasn't that the Bowen man? Why, they wondered, had he come back after so long? It could only mean trouble.

A dust-devil whirled up the main street and Pete winced his eyes against the dust-driven grit, unbuttoned his long grimy mackinaw and loosened his heavy .44s in their bear-greased holsters on either hip, before pushing into the cantina. It was crowded with Mexicans. One or two glanced up at this hombre, nervously. They did not reply to his nod of greeting, but watched him, furtively. Black Pete found himself a seat at a table and ordered himself a jug of water and a plate of enchiladas. The people at his table quickly finished their meal and moved out of his way.

Pete shrugged, took his hat off, and sank the water, fresh with ice from the mountains, until his thirst was quenched. Then he got stuck into the enchiladas: tortillas of thin pancake bread dipped in chillie sauce and piled one on top of another, with chopped onions and grated cheese sprinkled between the layers. The whole appetising pile was crowned with two fried eggs.

Sweat began to prick out on Pete's brow and rivulet down his neck. It sure was good to get back to parts where they knew how to cook after all them bland dishes of the north: so hot, it was stripping the lining out of his throat.

'Mighty fahn,' he said, after enjoying a hot coffee and paying his bill. 'Mebbe I'll jest take a small joy juice.'

First, though, he walked over to the bank. Again it fell silent as the tall rider in his mackinaw entered. He was bearded, his hair uncut, hanging over his collar, and he could well have been some bank robber or other ne'er-do-well. But, there were sly nudges as they recognized him, especially when he took a wad of greenbacks out of his coat, paid $3,000 into his account.

In the stores he bought a black lace mantilla for Louisa. It would do nicely for their rare excursions to the town church. And a pair of silver-plated spurs to fit Jim. Again nobody answered his greeting, merely watched him, suspiciously. Or, what was it, a mingling of malice and pity in their eyes? It sure made him uneasy.

In fact, he had begun to get that feeling he sometimes got before a gunfight, or before going into battle – an emptiness in his lungs, his heart thudding in its cage, a sense of being 'out of his body', watching himself from elsewhere – as he packed his parcels away on his tired horse, and, straight-backed, and broad-shouldered, walked over to the saloon. A voice whispered to him that this was not a good idea, but it was as if he was hypnotized, impelled to walk over there. He was being waited for....

The sun was going down behind his back, splitting itself and bleeding over the mountains, and tumbleweed was blowing along the wide dusty street. He had forgotten how unfriendly this town could be. Shimmering curtains of red sunlight flickered their rays across the broad valley like the final wave of some drowning swimmer. And old men, sat in rocking chairs on the sidewalk, started as they saw him: a dark threatening figure. He seemed to have appeared out of nowhere.

Pete pushed through the wooden doors of the saloon and stood there dark against the red sky, his eyes probing the gloom. They were ranged along the bar, back by the card tables, up along the bare plank wall, silent, as if waiting for him, facing him, some dozen of them.

'*Buenos dias, señor,*' the barkeep said, breaking the silence. Pete glanced at him. It was a different man.

'*Buenos,*' he murmured, stepping over to the bar. 'Gimme a tequila.'

Carefully, deliberately, he took off his leather gloves, tipped salt on to his bare knuckle, taking a lick, as he tossed the tequila back. He took half a lemon from the bar, bit his teeth into it, taking a squeeze. Its sharp sourness gave his mind a sharpness, too. But, it was still as if he were in another world, everything clearly outlined, taking on a new meaning, the drops of moisture on the bottle, the flies dancing aimlessly in the air, even the beads of sweat on the barkeep's upper lip, his scared-rabbit eyes, the slight movement of his hand towards a shotgun beneath the counter. 'I'd advise you to keep out of it,' Pete muttered, and turned to the men.

He pulled his mackinaw apart to reveal the butts of his well-used .44s jutting forward on either hip. Vaguely he recognized some of the men: Rocky Mountain Mars, a well-known braggart, standing beside Hal Murchison, Red-nosed Frank, Parson Cates, Sourside Mason, Johnny Silver, Biglips George: a mix of petty criminals, hired killers and cowpokes. And Slim McKenzie, his long-chinned narrow face, a shadow at the far end of the hall.

'You been away a long time,' McKenzie's voice rang out, 'what you come back for?'

'Yeah,' Hal blustered, 'Doncha know you ain't wanted around here?'

'You the welcoming committee?' Pete forced a smile and slowly lit a cheroot, gritting his brownstained teeth on the stub. 'Why should I give a damn what you want?'

'It ain't jest us who don't wancha, Bowen,' Hal Murchison sneered. 'It's your wife who don't wancha? Dincha know?'

'What you say?' Pete whispered, sucking the black smoke into his lungs – it was as if the words were an arrow that had entered his heart and the men were dark silent mourners watching him die.

There was such a glint in his narrowed eyes that Hal raised his open hands, stuttering, 'You cain't shoot me, I ain't armed.'

'Waal,' Pete whispered, pulling back his coat further, 'you fat slopbucket, git yourself a gun.'

'He don't need one,' McKenzie said, stepping forward, 'I got one here.'

'Cain't he fight his own battles? You his nursemaid?'

They looked at each other, venomously, as the men began to back out of the way. Pete saw the thin figure in his tight trousers and tall fancy black boots, the silk waistcoat, behind which lay the susceptible throbbing heart, the organs behind the skin which he had to lay waste, put an end to. It was as if he could see his skeleton behind the clean shirt, the bootlace tie, the cadaverous grey shaven jaw. It was as if he could see *everything*. It was one of those moments when time stands still.

Slim flicked aside his coat to reveal the Colt Frontier revolver, a silver-embossed expensive model, and there was a flicker of a smile on his lips, a not unfriendly glimmer in his eye. This argument, after all, had little to do with him. They were merely two fighters, two shootists, two of the best, forced finally to meet. It was inevitable.

Black Pete met his eyes and remembered Carson's words: 'Take your time. Every gunfighter has his time. If he tries to beat his time he'll miss. Try for a heart shot'....

He saw Slim's eyes darken with the coldness of death, saw him begin to make his move: Pete's long fingers shot across to his left hip like a whiplash and his .44 was out and grasped firm in his hand. He was stepping aside, crouching over, as McKenzie's shot crashed out, singeing his ear. Pete aimed, for a fraction of a second, just long enough, before McKenzie could pull another bullet, and fired: BLAM! He had aimed at the belt buckle, as he always did, the recoil of his big gun slamming the slug up: but it was a surprise, as it always was, to see it smash a hole in McKenzie's chest.

Slim stood there, staring, stupidly, as if he could not believe it, that this could not be happening, trying to steady his revolver for another shot.

Black Pete clenched his teeth and squeezed again, his second bullet hitting the lucky golden dollar dangling from McKenzie's satin vest: CRASH! knocking him backwards to the floor. Blood had begun to seep from the hole in his shirt and he looked at a handful of it as if it could not be his. Again he struggled to aim his revolver, but it clattered from his hands. 'You ... you....' There was something he wanted to say, but he couldn't get it out. A flood of blood poured from his mouth and he collapsed prone, his life draining out of him.

'He drew too fast,' Pete muttered, as if to himself. 'He misjudged it.'

There was a smell in the air as if the place had been hit by a thunderbolt. A smell of death and gunsmoke you never forgot. The men did not speak, but, after staring at the stricken McKenzie for a few moments, with one accord they clattered out of the saloon. They leaped on to their horses and hit leather, out toward the Murchison range.

Pete poked McKenzie with his boot. 'Sorry, Slim,' he whispered. 'Nothing personal.'

He turned back to the bar. 'Gimme another drink,' he said. 'I need it.'

He had to get out of there. Had to get back to his wife and family. Something bad was festering in the back of his mind. He had to see what had been going on. Even if he was afraid of what that might be.

He rode out of town, out across the empty plain, the scent of gunsmoke still in his nostrils, out towards the harsh Mountains of Death. The sky was a blaze of glory, the colour of fire, the crimson of blood.

TWENTY-SIX

Sombrero Rock was a black silhouette against a pink-flushed sky of dawn as Pete rode towards his ranch house. He noticed things that were different, fences that had been fixed. An ominous sense of foreboding came over him.

He dumped his saddle and gear in the dust and let the horse loose in the corral. He saw the grey filly, who came trotting towards him, whickering, her hooves thudding in the quiet of early morning. She had grown tall and filled out. She would have gotten too big for Jim, unless his legs, too, had stretched. She had become a man's horse. And she recognized the man who had first tamed her, and nuzzled his palm, licking at the salt.

He felt apprehensive, a light sweat had broken out on him, and his heart was thudding in his ribcage, thudding in his mind like the sound of an Indian drum. Something, he knew, was not as it ought to be. He walked over to the rough ranch house, through its open door, across the hardened mud floor of the kitchen and eating-room. He unlatched the door of their bedroom.

Estevan sat up with sudden realization, his dark slim body naked, his eyes staring, vividly violet beneath his mop of curls. Louisa, too, gave a gasp of dismay, and backed away against the bedhead, snatching at the sheet to cover her bare breasts from her husband's fierce eyes.

'What 'n hell's goin' on?' Pete whispered, hoarsely, and knew, at the back of his mind it was a foolish question. It was obvious what had been going on but he could yet hardly believe it.

Estevan's fingers began to reach for the Navy Colt in its holster on the belt of bullets hung on the iron corner post of the bed.

'I wouldn't do that,' Pete said, deliberately drawing his right-hand .44, clicking the hammer back. He could hear the clucking of chickens outside, the haloo of a rooster; he could see the sun's rays filtering through the planks, turning the room crimson, the start of what might have been a wonderful day. And the sweat had turned cold on his body as he shivered and his finger pressed the trigger.

'Don't!' Louisa screamed, kneeling up, as if to throw herself in front of him.

Pete pulled his left-hand .44 and pointed it at her. He felt a terrible fear, as if his whole world was falling away from him, as if he were sliding into a pit, a pit of loneliness and shame that would be forever with him.

'I ought to kill you, too, as well as this slimy snake.'

'Go on,' she said, kneeling, her hair straggling over her liquid eyes, as if facing a firing squad. 'I don' blame you.'

'It's not Louisa's fault,' Estevan said. 'You shouldn't have left us here.'

Pete couldn't help an embittered gasp of laughter coming from his lips. 'You durn right I shouldn't have left you here.' He released the pressure on the trigger. 'Get outside. Get out of my durn bed.'

Estevan pulled on his tight leather trousers, his embroidered shirt, tentatively took his gunbelt from the bed, strapped it across his chest. 'You want to fight fair outside? I will be waiting for you.'

He heard his son speaking in the kitchen. 'Hello, Estevan, what you doing?'

How could he kill his son's mother? Any other man in Texas might have done. But, he felt only dismay. How could he kill her lover? He even liked Estevan. The shock of finding them entwined together in his marital bed was too much to handle. He put his .44s away and sat on the bed edge, and his shoulders began to shudder.

Louisa put her fingers in the long hair at the nape of his neck and gently caressed him. 'Jim doesn't know,' she whispered. 'Estevan is usually gone by the time Jim gets up. It's been so long. I didn't know what had happened to you. I'm sorry.'

Pete had not wept in a long time. Not since he was a soldier in the War. That first terrible battle, Shiloh, when most of his comrades had been slaughtered. Now the tears began to silently trickle down his cheeks, and his body was racked with shudders. '*Why?*' he said.

'It was hearing about you and Molly. It did somethin' to me. I thought you had gone to find her again. I tried, but I couldn't hold out.'

'Molly?' He groped for words. 'She ... I ...'

She soothed him like a mother a child. Gradually he pulled himself together. He wasn't going to kill Estevan. She knew that. Jim suddenly burst in and shouted, 'Pa!' and had his arms around his neck, and Pete was blinking, and smiling, through his tears.

'I found these outside,' Jim said, waving the silver spurs. 'Are these for me?'

'Sure,' Pete said. He did not mention the mantilla for Louisa. He knew only the huge chasm that had suddenly opened between them.

'Leave your father alone,' Louisa urged. 'He is exhausted from travelling. He needs to rest.'

She ushered the boy out, and quickly dressed. She, too, was in a state of shock. She did not know what to do. Could it be possible that she loved both of these men? Could it be possible to live with two husbands? In a state of polygamy? Like the Mormons, but in a reverse way? She could not envisage not seeing either of them again. She pressed Pete to lay back on their bed, pulled his boots off, went to make him coffee. When she returned he was propped up, staring into space, but he turned his dark eyes to burn upon her. 'What are you going to do?'

'I don't know. We will have to talk about it. Estevan has taken Jim out to herd in some horses off the range. We will talk about it tonight. I think you should sleep now.'

'I don't wanna sleep,' Pete said. 'Jest tell me. You want me to go?'

'It's not fair,' she said, and blurted out, 'Couldn't we all stay together?'

Pete shook his head, and smiled at her. 'Louisa, I never thought I'd ever think you were crazy. What do we do? Have you alternate nights? Or all in together?'

Somehow, being able to smile about it made it

seem not so bad. And he did feel terrible tired. He
hadn't slept properly for days, or weeks, and
certainly not in a bed, under cover. Or maybe she
had put something in that coffee, but he felt a
huge lassitude gripping him, and, as he sank back
on the bed, he felt her lips gently kiss him, her
tears fall on his face, as he slipped into darkness.

He woke to the sound of the earth drumming.
And, instead of the darkness of his sleep, it was
already the darkness of night, and through the
chink in the planks he could see the shadowy
shapes of horsemen coming and they had burning
torches in their hands. For moments he thought
that he was dreaming, or that they were the
Horsemen of the Apocalypse.

He was up on his bare feet and reaching for his
guns, stumbling out into the kitchen, past Louisa,
who had a rifle in her hands, her face aghast. he
pushed her behind him and signalled her to stay,
and ran out into the yard as the horsemen
charged, leaping across the barricades they had
erected against the Comanches. The air was full
of the sound of gunfire, of leather harness, of
screaming horses, full of swirling dust.

Estevan was crouched behind the wagon, his
Navy revolver raised. He took two men out of
their saddles. Pete joined him, firing two-handed,
his .44s blazing, bringing more men down. Up in
the stable loft where he had been playing, Jim
fired his rifle, doing his part. A burning brand was
tossed into the stable door and with a crackling of
dry timbers the whole lot began to go up. The
house, too, was on fire.

'Get Louisa out,' he shouted to Estevan. 'I'm

going for Jim.'

He stood and saw a masked man wearing a piebald vest bearing down upon him and knew it was George Murchison. He aimed his last slug at his leather vest and saw him tumble from the saddle, his waist flowing blood.

Pete dashed for the stable, a panic in him, but it was already a maelstrom of smoke and flames. He could not find the boy anywhere, only plaintively bellowing cows, and chickens flapping foolishly as they roasted to death. A timber beam crashed down, and he was forced to step back into the yard, a panic terror in his mind.

Estevan was backing up to the house, but in the doorway he fell to one knee, clutching at his lead-pierced heart; his handsome young face a retch of horror, as he staggered back into the doorway of the building, which was now burning furiously.

The men howled and yipped and rode around. There were too many of them and they had murder on their minds. Pete saw Hal Murchison, fat-chested, on his horse, his broken-nosed face gleaming red in the flames, and he snatched up a carbine and blasted him, viciously.

He didn't have time to finish him off, because they were all around him. He turned to try to fight his way back into the stable, but a rope had snaked around his shoulders, and another, and he was being dragged away, and trampled on. Men pulled him to his feet, and he lashed out, kicking and punching with desperate strength, but they tightened the ropes around him, and he was held, helpless.

He stood and watched the horror of his house

like a burning pyre crashing down upon his wife and Estevan.

'You wouldn't be told!' The younger Murchison brother was holding his wounded side and screaming at him. His men were supporting him, picking up their injured and dead and loading them on to their horses, and preparing to ride back into the night as swiftly as they had come.

'Hang him high, boys. Let everyone know The Stranglers have ridden tonight,' young Murchison managed to shout as he was borne away with his stricken brother.

They snaked a noose over Pete's head, lifted him up, bodily, to sit on a horse, and, with wild cries, led him over to the entrance gateway over which a Wild Rose was proudly painted. One of the men shinned up to tie the rawhide rope securely to the top crossbar, lit by the flames.

'So long, Bowen,' one shouted. 'See you in hell.'

He savagely quirted the horse, which dashed away, leaving Black Pete dangling and kicking on the rope, the pain of the noose searing into his throat.

The men watched for a few moments and laughed, as they trailed away into the night.

TWENTY-SEVEN

Jim peeped out from the dairy where he had been hiding. He had his tomahawk in his hand ready to fight any of the enemy who were around. He saw the silhouette against dancing fire: a man, his arms bound, his legs kicking, hanging from a rope. He raced across. He sobbed when he saw it was his father. He knew he had been lynched. He climbed up to the crossbar and hacked at the rope with his tomahawk. His father's eyes were bulging and his tongue was sticking out, going blue. Horrible. The last strand broke and he hit the ground.

'Pa,' Jim cried. 'Are you OK? Say something, Pa.'

The boy pulled out Pete's knife and cut through his bonds. Pete reached up clutching fingers and loosened the noose around his neck, his eyes flickering open. His mouth croaked but he could form no words. He lay looking at the stars until he could summon his strength. And he crawled to his feet.

'Where's mother?' the boy whimpered. 'Where's Estevan?'

They went over to look at the burning house: its last posts suddenly crumbled into a mass of fiercely-glowing cinders. Pete put his arm around the boy's shoulder and hugged him. 'They've gone,' he whispered, his voice hardly audible. 'They're dead. They've gone together. They've found peace.'

'Why, Pa?' – he heard the boy's voice, as if from a far distance – 'Why did they do it, Pa?'

'I dunno,' he croaked, a beaten man. 'Greed. Pure greed. I should never have come back here.'

'But why did they kill mother? She never hurt anyone.'

'I don't know. I jest don't know. She was a true, good, woman. I wish it could have been me instead. I wish she had taken you away.'

His first instinct was to ride over to the Murchison ranch and attack them, vindictively and with vengeance in his soul, as they had attacked him. But he feared for the safety of the boy.

In the morning, after he had buried the bloody charred remains, with the help of the Concho woman, and erected two wooden crosses, he saddled up the grey filly for himself, and a pony for Jim. He took a long last look back at Sombrero Rock, and taking a string of spare horses, set off across the plain.

His neck was red raw and sore and it was painful to speak. He guessed he would recover. The durn fools had put the knot of the rope in the wrong position. It had to go under the left side of the jaw for, as the noose gyrates clockwise through a quarter circle, the rope has to end up under the chin to throw the neck back and snap the spinal column. They had put the knot on the right side of the jaw and it had swung to the back

of the neck and thrown his head forward. In those
few seconds, dangling between death and life, he
had almost choked to death. If his son hadn't
saved him he would have done. His neck had not
broken.

He was surprised he could think about these
matters so calmly as they wended their way
towards the north. It was as if his whole life had
fallen away from him. As if he were floating in a
vast vacuum. As if nothing mattered any more.
There were only two things of importance: to get
his boy to safety, and to avenge Louisa. He had
helped to hang men before. Those had been legal
executions. The execution he planned to carry out
would be an illegal one – of the man responsible
for these terrible events.

It took a long time to reach San Antonio. Once
there he put Jim on the stagecoach for Kansas
City. He had already telegraphed Louisa's sister
in that town and informed her of what had
occurred. She had replied that she would be glad
to bring the boy up as her own. He had the bank
forward her his $3,000 in capital.

As he shook Jim's hand and urged him to be
brave, Pete did not want to let him go. Maybe he
should get on to the stage with him, find a new
life, forget all this? But his bitterness and desire
for revenge had become like a burning fixation in
his mind. He owed it to Louisa, he told himself. He
wondered, afterwards, if that were true, whether
she would have wanted him to take the law into
his own hands? But Jim was giving him a cheerful
smile and a wave and the stage was pulling out.
He was left standing in the town square. Alone.

More alone than he had ever been before.

The Texas Cattlemen's Club was an imposing building set back out of town on a piece of parkland. It had three storeys, and was built of wood, stone and iron, with a wide veranda all around it. As he rode his horse up to it he could see several 'gentlemen' sat in wicker armchairs on the veranda, doing their deals or reminiscing. You had to be one of a handpicked membership of 200 to drink here. You could guzzle fine wines, brandies, sherries and champagne. You could gorge on caviar and French cooking: if you happened to be a cattle baron. The gentlemen on the veranda looked askance at this *hombre* who dismounted, hitched his reins to one of the iron pillars, and climbed the steps to the main entrance. Black Pete recognized one of them as Shanghai Pierce, an uncouth blackguard, who had grabbed control of more than a million acres. He directed his query at him. 'Is Abraham Murchison here?'

'Yeah,' said Pierce, suave in his citified clothes. 'Last saw him in the smoking-room.'

'Where's that?'

'Through past the dining-room. Is something wrong? You cain't just walk in –'

Pete ignored him, as he ignored the cries of the reception clerk, the *maitre d'hotel*, and others who challenged this dark stranger, his face set grim, in his grimy mackinaw and jingling spurs, clomping across the polished hardwood floors, past the tables laid with sparkling cloths and silver. There was something awesome about the way he pushed through them, as if propelled by an unknown dark force.

His heart was thumping in his chest, as it had thumped that morning he had returned to the ranch; and his mind was full of images, Louisa kneeling on the bed, the barn and house burning, the whirling horses, the cursing men, the rope tearing into his windpipe, the cinder-black and bloody red bodies he had buried.

He saw a group of men, evil old men who ran America, greybeards, in frock coats and loose bow ties, sat in armchairs. And he met the startled frown of the gaunt, eagle-faced Abraham Murchison. He was struggling to get to his feet, to back away, but there was nowhere he could run to. Murchison was not wearing a gun, but Pete did not care. He was going to kill him, anyway. He slowly drew out his Smith and Wesson in his right hand, slowly pointed it at the old man, slowly cocked it, and waited for some seconds ... time seemed to stand still ... the men in the armchairs were a rigid frieze.

'Remember me?' he whispered, and saw Murchison's lips quiver. A silent pleading. The explosion seemed to come from far off. Murchison had fallen back into his armchair. There was a hole in his forehead from which blood was trickling. He was dead.

Black Pete turned on his heel and strode back through the club, with its oil paintings and antlers on the walls, its plush carpets and grand staircases, and men stood and stared at him as if he were a ghost, not daring to intervene. He held the heavy smoking revolver hanging at his side and went through them, unseeing. He carefully untied his grey, climbed into the saddle, and rode away, his back ramrod straight, as if he were setting off on a military mission.

He rode out of San Antonio and kept on riding. From here on he would be a hunted man. An outlaw. Black Pete, Outlaw, they would call him.

STOCK CIRCULATION

CUF 7/02 BOX			